Wish

Upon a Crawdad

Wish
Upon a Crawdad

Curtis W. Condon

*Heart of Oak Books
for Young Readers*

Cover illustration by Francisco Villa
Edited by Jennifer Paton

Publisher's Cataloging-In-Publication Data
Condon, Curtis W., author.
Wish Upon a Crawdad / by Curtis W. Condon.
[Forest Grove, Oregon] : Heart of Oak Books for Young Readers, [2022] | Interest age level: 9-12.
ISBN 979-8-9852234-0-8 (paperback)
Mothers and daughters—Oregon—Juvenile fiction. | Electricity—Oregon—History—20th century—Juvenile fiction. | Farm life—Oregon—Juvenile fiction. | Friendship—Juvenile fiction. | Courage—Juvenile fiction.
LCC PZ7.1.C6459 Wi 2022 (print) | LCC PZ7.1.C6459 (ebook) | DDC [E]--dc23

Library of Congress Control Number: 2021953436

Printed in the United States of America

*To my mother, Lois Condon,
whose fingerprints appear
throughout this book.*

TABLE OF
CONTENTS

Afterword: A Few More Things

About the Author: Curtis W. Condon

Wish

Upon a Crawdad

Chapter 1

DISASTER IN DISGUISE

I will never forget that terrible sight for as long as I live. One minute, Momma's vase was sitting on the shelf above the kitchen window, and the next minute it was tumbling in midair toward the floor.

The crystal vase usually came down from its lofty perch only on special occasions. It was one of Momma's most precious possessions.

Great-granddad had made the vase the day Grandma Flynn was born. He gave it to her on her wedding day, and she brought it with her on the boat to America and passed it down to Momma when she married Daddy. I suppose my sister, Patsy, or I would have been next in line to receive it.

That may explain why I tried so hard to make a diving catch to save it. Unfortunately, I'm no Joe DiMaggio. The vase slipped off my fingertips, and I watched helplessly as it shattered on the floor in front of me.

When I looked up at Momma, she was brandishing a frying pan, poised to strike. Her face was red and contorted with anger. I had never, ever seen her so mad.

Which got me thinking …

Some folks went looking for trouble. They knew what they were doing was wrong before they did it. Not me. Not this time. Trouble came looking for Ruby Mae Ryan, and I didn't have a clue why. In fact, the afternoon had started so innocently.

I was minding my own business. The crawdad business that is. I was stretched out alongside the creek catching crawdads for a customer when someone snuck up behind me.

"Hey! Whatcha doing?" they bellowed, giving me a start.

Drat! It was my little brother, Marty. I wanted to ignore him, but I was sure he saw me jump. No doubt he would keep bothering me if I didn't say something.

"What does it look like I'm doing?" I snapped.

Marty was two years younger than me. He was the baby of the family, but even he knew better than to bother me when I had a crawdad sniffing my bait.

The creek was shallow and clear enough to see the crawdad tiptoeing on spiny legs. It was the color of a rusty railroad spike. The scent of the raw bacon tied to the chicken-wire bottom of my jerry-rigged net brought the crawdad right to me.

It was the first crawdad of the day. I always made a wish on the first one, just like folks who wished on the first star at night. I did that too, but I figured my odds were better with crawdads. Not many folks wished upon a crawdad.

That might sound silly, but it worked. My wish for electricity was proof of that. It was coming true this summer when the co-op brought electricity to the valley for the very first time.

My new wish was to earn enough money to buy something extraordinary. I didn't like to say out loud what it was, though, because that might jinx the wish, and then it would never come true.

I had just made my wish when a rock splashed in the creek out of nowhere. It sent a geyser into the air and ripples rolling across the water. I lost sight of the crawdad for a moment, but then caught a glimpse of reddish-brown squirting into the weeds along the bank.

"Why did you do that?" I demanded, jumping up, ready for a fight.

Even at ten years old, Marty was bigger than me—just about everybody was—but I stood toe-to-toe, glaring up at him. He wore a smug, goofy grin that I wanted to wipe off his face.

My fists relaxed when I noticed what he had squeezed to his chest. It was a kitten, not more than eight or nine months old. The sight of it made me go soft inside.

The ball of fur had a beautiful gray-brown, spotted-tabby coat, amber eyes, and pointy tufts of hair on the tips of each ear. It was just about the cutest thing I'd ever seen.

The kitten was wrapped in what looked like a ratty, burlap baby blanket.

"What's with the gunnysack?" I asked.

"To keep from getting scratched."

"Oh. Can I hold him?"

"No," Marty said flatly. "And for your information, it's not a him. It's a her."

The kitten kept squirming, trying to get away. It didn't like Marty much. Can't say I blamed the poor thing.

"Don't hold her so tight," I said.

"I have to, Ruby. Otherwise, she'll get away."

"She can hardly move and that scares her."

I started to pet the kitten. At first, she paid no mind and continued to struggle, but soon she calmed down and seemed to enjoy the attention. She especially liked being scratched around the ears, pushing her head against my fingers.

After a while, the kitten stopped struggling and began to purr. She opened and closed her eyes lazily as if nodding off to sleep.

"Where did you find her?"

"Out by the slaughter block."

Ick! That was where Daddy and the older boys butchered chickens for supper.

"She was watching me from the edge of the woods. Looked friendly enough, so I caught her."

"Doesn't seem to like you now."

"She likes me fine, thank you very much," Marty said, his voice growing louder.

"Okay. Okay. I didn't mean anything by it," I said, afraid his loud mouth would upset the kitten. "How'd you coax her out?"

A smile spread across his face. "I got a rag and rubbed it on the slaughter block to pick up chicken smell, and then I waved it in the air so she could get a good whiff. Wasn't long and out she came," Marty said. "Pretty smart, huh?"

"Sure. Smart," I said, shining him on. "How 'bout you let me hold her a while?"

Marty passed me the kitten as if it were a newborn baby.

"It's okay, kitty," I said, baby talking.

I no sooner had the kitten when Marty snickered. He tried to pretend he didn't, but his grin was a dead giveaway.

"Hey, what's up?"

"Nothing," he said, on the verge of laughing. "I'm just wondering how you're gonna get Momma to let you keep the kitten."

I looked at him suspiciously. "Who says I'm going to ask?"

"I do. I can tell you're attached to that cat already."

I hated to admit it, but Marty was right. I fell in love the minute I saw her. I even had the perfect name: Princess.

"I suppose I'll appeal to Momma's motherly instincts," I said. "After all, we can't leave this poor, abandoned kitty to survive in the wild on her own."

I headed for the house.

"I've gotta see this," Marty said, tagging along.

We walked along the creek, then across the farmyard. As we headed up the hill toward the house, the cows followed. Our horses, Rickabar and Hercules, were already waiting for us at the ends of their paddocks. Rickabar leaned over the fence, his ears up and pointed toward us. He put his muzzle high in the air to get a sniff of Marty, me, and the kitten as we passed.

Our dog, Laddie, bounded up to us, curious about the ball of fur and burlap plastered to my chest. When he caught the scent of cat, he started to bark and circle.

The kitten instinctively curled into a tighter ball, arching its back as it watched Laddie carrying on.

"Be quiet!" I yelled.

It was no use. Laddie seemed possessed and kept right on following and barking.

As Marty and I clamored up the back porch steps, Laddie sunk his teeth into a dangling corner of the gunnysack and started to pull.

"Let go!" I yelled as I steadied myself on the top step.

I tried to pull back, but it was no use. Laddie ripped the gunnysack away. He growled and shook it violently like I'd seen him do to opossums and wood rats after catching them.

I hugged the kitten to my chest and sprinted across the porch and into the kitchen. The screen door slapped shut behind me. The sound took me by surprise. I thought Marty would be there to catch the door on his way in. But he wasn't. He had disappeared.

I suddenly felt uneasy. Maybe it wasn't such a good idea after all. Momma didn't exactly approve of me bringing home strays.

She was stoking the cookstove for supper. A kettle of water sat on top, not yet steaming. The kitchen air had a hint of smoke, mixed with the lingering smell of fried ham from breakfast.

On the island behind Momma was the big mixing bowl.

The flour tin sat beside it, along with a plate of chicken, eggs, salt, and a few other ingredients. My mouth watered. She was making my favorite: chicken and noodles.

"What are you kids up to?" she asked, without turning around.

I could have changed my mind. I could have answered, "Oh, nothing," and left without saying another word. I probably should have. But I couldn't help myself.

"Look what Marty found."

Momma gave no indication she heard me. She was too busy coaxing the fire. When she finished, she went to the sink and pumped water to wash her hands.

"What's that you've got, Ruby?" she asked, smiling softly as she walked toward me, drying her hands.

"It's a kitten, Momma."

Her smile turned upside down. "Now, you know your daddy and I said no more animals."

I thought she might say that, so I had a plan to win her over. How could she say no once she saw the pretty kitty or felt its thick, soft fur?

"Here," I said, offering the kitten to Momma. "Don't you want to at least hold it?"

I could tell Momma was curious. She loved kittens as much as I did, but as she came closer, a flurry of emotions—surprise, confusion, then anger—flashed across her face.

"You get that bobcat out of here, this minute!" she ordered, pointing to the door.

Bobcat? How could that be? Sure, it had the right colors and markings, but it didn't have a bobcat's distinctive tail. Or did it?

I took a quick look. Sure enough. With the gunnysack gone, I could see its stubby tail. I turned toward the door and saw Marty through the screen. He was peeking around the corner, wearing that stupid grin again.

That's when Laddie came bounding and barking through the house from the opposite direction.

The bobcat let out a yowl. It hissed and spat as Laddie came to a stop in front of me. He was barking up a storm as if he had treed a raccoon.

The bobcat tried desperately to get away. It was all I could do to hold on. Its claws poked through my blouse and scratched me. It hurt so bad and the bobcat squirmed so violently that she squirted out of my grip.

She clawed up to my shoulder, then leaped onto Momma. It happened so fast and unexpectedly that Momma reacted as if she'd been splashed with a bucket of cold water.

"Scat!" she yelled without thinking.

Momma attempted to grab the bobcat, missed, and nearly slapped herself in the face trying.

The bobcat clung to Momma's shoulder only long enough to get its bearings, then launched itself toward the shelf above the stove. Unfortunately, the bobcat didn't make it and landed smack-dab on the top of the stove. It wasn't red-hot, but it was warm enough to give her a scare.

The poor thing jumped straight up and howled something awful, more surprised than hurt. It landed on the floor near Laddie but bounded onto the nearest counter before the dog could react.

The bobcat was out of her mind with fear. She dashed around the kitchen with abandon, knocking over everything in her path, looking for a way to escape or a place to hide.

She bounded over the mixing bowl and landed on the bowl of eggs. The bowl clattered to the floor, surviving its fall, but splattering eggs everywhere. The flour was next to be knocked over, sending a cloud of white billowing into the air.

The bobcat crisscrossed the kitchen so fast that she was impossible to catch. All the while, Laddie, Momma, and I kept bumping into each other as we chased her. The scene would have made a matinee audience roar with laughter. In real life, it wasn't the least bit funny.

At some point, Momma armed herself with a pot and frying pan. I don't know what she meant to do with them. She wouldn't hurt a fly. But there she was, running around the kitchen in a haze of flour dust with a frying pan in one hand and a saucepan in the other, red-faced and screaming like a crazy woman.

That's when the bobcat jumped on the shelf above the kitchen window. She stopped, turned, and looked down at us. She was breathing hard. Her back was arched, her nubby tail sticking straight up. Then she let out a hiss that made me shiver.

Laddie took it as a challenge. He nearly jumped into the sink trying to get at the bobcat, which sent her running across the shelf, knocking over everything in her path, including Momma's crystal vase. The vase spun in slow, wobbly circles toward the edge of the shelf. Then it fell.

The crash of the vase breaking was the last straw for the terrified bobcat. She dove from her high perch, ricocheted off the counter down to the floor, and hit the screen door at full speed.

The impact didn't make the door swing open, but it was enough to make it move a little. The bobcat jammed a paw into the opening, then her head. It took all her strength to squeeze the rest of her body through and escape.

Laddie wasn't about to let the bobcat get away. He jumped on the screen door with both front paws, slamming it open, and continued the chase outside.

It was suddenly quiet in the kitchen, all except for the sound of Laddie's distant barking. Flour still hung in the air. The room was a total disaster, with wet and dry messes everywhere.

Momma was frozen like a statue, the pot and frying pan still in her hands. She looked hurt and dazed, like when I stepped on a rake and its handle flew up and clonked me in the head.

Her gaze was fixed on the shattered pieces of her precious vase. She shut her eyes and squeezed them tight. When she opened them again, they were filled with tears—and looking straight at me.

I held my breath, prepared for Momma to yell. But she didn't. She was much too mad to utter a single word.

Then, when I thought I couldn't hold my breath any longer, Momma turned and walked quietly out of the kitchen—pot, frying pan, and all. That's when I knew I was in more trouble than I had ever been in my whole life.

Chapter 2

BANISHED TO THE WHALE

Whenever I had thinking time, I liked to stand at my bedroom window and watch the world go by. At least I tried to. Truth be told, there was never much traffic on the valley road. The view was more like a picture postcard with mountains and trees.

It reminded me I'd rather be outside than inside, even on a rainy day. Especially in May, when the trees and plants were bursting with new green, and the air smelled so fresh and sweet.

But there I was, banished to my room without supper. Momma was so mad she barely talked to me all afternoon. However, five words she did say were, "You're grounded for a week."

Don't get me wrong. I don't mind spending time in my room. It's a special place to read and think and dream. But it's different when I don't have a choice in the matter. Besides, the only thing I could think of now was poor Momma's shattered vase.

I flopped on my bed and stared into space. There wasn't a ceiling, so what I saw were the exposed beams and rafters holding up the roof. I used to lay there and pretend I was inside a whale. The boards were the whale's ribs, and my window was its mouth.

What would it be if I pretended tonight? A prison cell maybe, with only a narrow bed, a dresser, a nightstand, and my few belongings.

Oh yeah, and a bedpan under the bed, which was just a fancy name for a bucket. It was there for when it was too cold or rainy to run to the outhouse. I didn't like to use it, though. It made too much noise.

I pulled a wad of paper out of my pocket. It was the list of chores Momma gave me as punishment for the bobcat fiasco. The list was long, but not so terrible. Most everything on it was chores I usually did anyway, just not all at once in a week.

One chore I wasn't looking forward to was cleaning up Daddy's wiring messes. They were all over the house, now that electricity was coming soon.

Daddy had cut holes in the walls for electric outlets. That's what made the messes. Bits of plaster and lattice on the floor here and there marked his trail.

Plaster dust was the worst. It settled on everything and kept coming back no matter how often it was dusted off.

At least Daddy didn't have to wire the lights. He and Grandpa had done that before the depression started, back when they thought electricity was coming once before. But the power line only got as far as Crossroads and stopped.

The thing I dreaded the very most on Momma's list was doing the wash. Not just wringing out the clothes and hanging them to dry, as I always did on Monday afternoons, but also hand washing and rinsing the laundry. Momma usually did that.

That explained why her hands were so ugly. Don't get me wrong. Momma was the prettiest woman around. Lots of folks said so. But her hands? Ugh! They were forever red, chapped, and cracked because of the awful laundry soap.

I used to be embarrassed by Momma's hands. Then I noticed the hands of most valley women looked the same way. But it still made me sad for Momma.

Almost every Christmas, I got her lotion or some other gift for her hands. The gifts didn't always work so well, like the sleeping gloves guaranteed to make a woman's hands baby-soft overnight. They didn't.

Then there was the time I concocted my own hand lotion. What a disaster!

I got the idea from Daddy. Sort of. He said the sheep buyer bragged about having the softest hands in the county because of handling sheep all day.

That gave me an idea: Why not make a lotion with sheep fat in it? So, I did.

The sheep fat didn't smell so good, so I added lemon juice and dried, ground geranium, chamomile, and rose, and mixed them all together. Then I put the concoction into an old cold crème jar.

The problem was sheep fat didn't age well in a jar. I had made the lotion the day after Thanksgiving, gift-wrapped it in an almost-new hanky, and then it sat in my dresser drawer or under the tree until Christmas.

When Momma opened it Christmas morning, the smell was so bad it almost knocked her over. The rest of us, too, but we didn't let on. All except Marty. He held his nose and made faces and disgusting noises.

Momma pretended not to notice. She scooped out some of the goo and rubbed it on her hands as if it were from Paris or someplace fancy like that.

I'll never forget that Christmas. Most likely, no one else will either. I don't know how long it took Momma to get the sheep fat off her hands, but the smell of it didn't go away for at least a week.

I caught myself smiling at the memory. It quickly faded when I remembered why I was in my room in the first place. I rolled over and buried my face in my pillow.

I had tried all kinds of distractions to forget my troubles: reading, drawing, practicing my penmanship. I even played a million games of jacks. Nothing seemed to help for very long.

I would have read more if the light was better, but daylight was fading. Too bad the electric lightbulb hanging from the rafter over my bed didn't work yet.

There had to be something I could do. I sat up and looked around my room.

My eyes settled on the small cloth bag on the dresser. Inside were the broken pieces of Momma's vase. I had picked them up before cleaning up the rest of the mess. I didn't know what I was going to do with them. I just knew they didn't belong down the outhouse pit with the rest of the rubbish.

Sitting beside the bag was my money jar. It was more than half full. It contained twelve dollars and thirty-eight cents. That much money could buy a lot of pretty things, but I was saving it for something special.

For the past two years, I had saved almost all my money. The jar contained mostly pennies, but there was a sprinkling of silver coins, too, including seven half-dollars and four silver dollars.

It had been a while since the last time the money was counted, so I got the jar and poured the coins on my bed. I always started with the silver dollars and worked my way down to the pennies.

"Why are you counting your money again?" whined a voice at the other end of the attic.

It was Marty. I couldn't see him, but I could hear him plain as day because we had flimsy curtains instead of doors hanging in the doorways to our rooms.

"I didn't know you were up here."

"I came up after mucking out the chicken coop. You were still cleaning the kitchen."

"Why'd you get sent to your room?"

"I got caught, same as you."

Well, I'll be darned. "That's news to me," I said.

"Oh, sure. You saw me on the porch. Momma did, too. Can't believe you didn't figure out that kitten was really a bobcat before it made such a mess."

"So, it *was* a trick!"

"Yeah, and boy did you fall for it."

I heard him chuckle.

"I'm sorry to hear you got in trouble," I said, my fingers crossed.

"Sure, you are," he scoffed.

"Well, just so you know, it wasn't me that squealed on you."

"I know. Momma figured I had something to do with it, and she told Daddy. He gave me a talking-to. And you know there's no lying to Daddy."

"Yeah, I know."

"He grounded me for a week. Came up with all kinds of extra chores."

I laughed.

"What's so funny?"

"Momma did the same to me."

I went on counting, putting the coins in piles by denomination.

"Ruby?"

"Yeah?"

"What are you going to do with all that money?"

"Spend it."

"On what? A new vase for Momma?" Marty joked.

It wasn't funny. Nothing hurt more than knowing I was partly responsible for Momma's broken vase. I didn't need to be reminded. I wanted to go over there and wring Marty's neck.

Marty kept right on talking. "You can't replace something like that," he said, his words cutting me deeper.

"You don't think I know that?"

"I'm just saying."

"Can we change the subject?"

"Sure. You never did tell me what you're going to buy."

"Something special."

"Yeah, but what?"

"Can't tell you. It's a secret."

It wouldn't be a secret very long if I told Marty. Only Daddy and my best friend, Virginia Valentine, knew what it was.

Just then, my stomach rumbled.

"Did you hear something?" Marty asked.

"Like what?"

"I thought I heard something growling. Sounded like the time we had raccoons in the wall."

I smiled. "Oh, that. That was me. I'm starving."

"Me too."

My stomach had been carrying on a one-way conversation all evening. I hadn't eaten a thing since noon, and the smells left over from supper didn't help.

"Ruby?"

"Yeah, Marty?"

"Can you stop counting? I want to go to sleep."

"Why so early?"

"What else am I going to do?"

"You could play solitaire or corner catch," I said, still counting my money. I tried to do it more quietly.

"No, I'm done. I just want to go to sleep."

His words struck a chord. Going to sleep and putting the day behind me didn't sound like such a bad idea. I started scooping up the coins and dumping them back into the jar.

"Ruby?"

"Go to sleep, Marty," I said, my stomach growling again. "I've stopped counting."

It was still twilight outside when everything was put away, and I settled in for the night. Usually, I wouldn't go to bed for another two hours, but I was ready for Saturday to be over. Thank goodness tomorrow was another day—and breakfast!

Chapter 3

HUNGRY AS A SPRING CHIPMUNK

I usually looked forward to sleeping in until seven-thirty on Sunday. It was my day off from chores, when I could lounge around like royalty until breakfast.

Not this Sunday. I was ready to get up an hour earlier and help Momma fix breakfast, not just for her sake but because I was hungry enough to eat Hamlet, Daddy's prize hog.

Momma was busy stoking the cookstove when I went out to the outhouse. She had the fire going and breakfast fixings laid out on the counter by the time I got back.

"Morning, Momma," I said in the sweetest voice I could muster.

"Morning, honey."

I breathed easier. Momma was still talking to me, despite everything that had happened the day before.

"You're up early for a Sunday."

I smiled at her as I washed my hands. "Yes, ma'am. I thought you could use a hand."

Momma's eyes narrowed. "Uh-huh."

"Scrambled eggs?" I asked, changing the subject.

"Yes, and biscuits and bacon, too."

Momma didn't have to say another word. I knew what to do. I'd been her helper six days a week since Patsy moved away to high school in Thackeray and then on to Portland to get a job and a different life.

I headed for the coop to feed the chickens and pick two dozen eggs. On the way back, I stopped at the smokehouse for bacon. I cut off an extra-big slab. There was no such thing as too much bacon.

When I got back to the house, Momma already had the biscuits in the oven, the wonderful smell starting to fill the kitchen and taunt my hunger. I tried not to think about it.

While Momma sliced the bacon into strips, I washed again and got things ready to make scrambled eggs once everything else was done.

Soon Momma had the bacon frying nice and slow. The smell was delicious, which only made my hunger pangs worse. My stomach felt like it had a squirrel running around inside, and it started to howl.

Momma looked up. "Did you say something?"

I shook my head. "No, ma'am." I didn't want to tell her it was my stomach growling. She might think I was whining.

Breakfast was well on its way, but it seemed an eternity before it was finally done, dished up, and everyone was seated around the table to say grace. Thankfully, Daddy made it a short prayer.

A mad dash followed. The bacon sat on the table in front of me, so I snatched my share before Bill, my oldest brother, could grab the plate. Marty was even faster at getting eggs.

"Now, now. Let's slow down," Daddy scolded, eyeing Marty, then me. "You'd think you haven't eaten in a week."

No, just eighteen hours, I thought to myself.

"Marty's trying to make up for lost time," Bill teased.

He held out the plate of biscuits to Marty. As Marty reached for one, Bill quickly pulled the plate away.

Marty rolled his eyes.

Bill offered the biscuits again. Marty snatched one before the plate could be pulled away again.

Daddy glanced at the boys, one of those quick, head-down looks. He knew kids would be kids and was a firm believer in letting them work things out for themselves, but he never let things get too out of hand.

Bill elbowed our other brother, Ed. "Hey, do you smell something?" he asked, obviously trying to start something.

Ed sniffed the air. "Why yes, yes I do."

"I thought so," said Bill, looking at Marty.

Marty noticed Bill's stare. "What?" he asked.

"You smell something?"

Marty sniffed the air. He thought about it, then sniffed his shirt.

"You smell it, don't you?" Bill insisted.

Marty squirmed. He had a bellyache look on his face. He got up from the table and was out of the dining room and halfway across the kitchen before he stopped, stood there a moment, then came back and sat down.

It was Momma's turn to take a quick, head-down glance around the table. She didn't have as much tolerance for kids being kids, especially when it came to the older boys picking on her baby.

"What's the matter, sport?" asked Ed.

Marty ignored him.

"Yeah. What's the matter?" Bill asked, piling on.

Marty's head snapped up. His face was red. "Ha-ha! Very funny, guys."

"What?" Bill asked innocently.

"These are my Sunday clothes. They ain't the ones I had on to clean the coop."

"Well, we smell something," Bill said, looking at Ed, who was nodding his head earnestly. "We think you do, too. Otherwise, why would you walk halfway back to your room after sniffing your shirt?"

Marty looked flustered.

"All right. Leave him be. That goes for Ruby, too," Daddy ordered. "Let them eat in peace."

Daddy took a hanky out of his back pocket and handed it to Marty. "Here. Blow your nose, son."

Anyone who had cleaned a chicken coop knew it took forever to get rid of the smell. It clung to your clothes, hair, skin, and those tiny, little hairs in your nose. That was the worst.

"Don't you blow your nose at the table," Momma said. She pointed to the kitchen. "Out there, and then wash your hands."

Breakfast was a quiet affair after that. The only sounds were forks on plates and Marty chewing a mile a minute with his mouth open.

I tried to eat slowly, to enjoy every tasty bite, but I couldn't help myself. I shoveled and chewed like there was no tomorrow. Before long, my plate was empty. I used the last bite of my second biscuit to wipe it clean.

When I looked up, I caught Daddy watching me. He grinned and gave me a wink.

It was no surprise Marty and I finished first. I can't speak for Marty, but I was still hungry. We had to watch as the others finished.

Everyone was dressed in their Sunday best. Momma and I wore neck-to-knees aprons to keep our dresses clean. It was the only day of the week I didn't mind wearing a dress, out of respect for the Lord.

As I watched Momma eat, it was hard to see why folks said

I looked like her. For one thing, she was pretty. I felt like an ugly duckling in comparison.

We did share fair skin and red hair. Mine was bright red. Momma's hair was more brownish-red. Auburn, she called it. But if I resembled Momma, it was in a short, skinny, freckle-splattered kind of way.

Daddy sure looked handsome in his white shirt and black necktie. The only things that looked out of place were his big, rough hands and the unbuttoned shirt cuffs because his wrists were too big around.

The boys were smaller versions of Daddy. They were tall and had his thick, dark hair and brown eyes. The only difference this morning was they wore bow ties instead of neckties.

"That was mighty tasty," Daddy said, pushing his plate away. He leaned back to stretch his stomach. "Thank you, Margaret."

Momma smiled softly and nodded at Daddy. She gathered the empty serving dishes and walked them to the sink.

"Ruby," Daddy began, "you clear the rest of the table and help your Momma with the dishes."

The boys were already moving. They knew what Daddy was going to say next. It was the same chores every Sunday morning.

"Bill, Ed, you two lock up the animals. Marty, you clean out the truck while I check the water and tire pressure," he said. "And don't get your clothes dirty. Any of you. You hear?"

There was a chorus of "Yes, Daddy" as we all hustled off in different directions to get ready for church.

Chapter 4

WHEN OLD FRIENDS COLLIDE

From one end to the other, the valley road was pocked with potholes. Daddy said weaving around them was like driving on the moon. Fortunately, he knew every hole from our farm to Crossroads, except the new ones that seemed to appear overnight.

"Watch out, James!" Momma yelled.

Daddy cranked the steering wheel hard to the right, but it was too late. The truck bucked and shuddered as the driver-side wheels took turns bottoming out in the pothole, and a splash of water flew up and spattered Daddy's window.

The boys bounced up and came down hard in the back of the truck. "Hey!" they shouted.

I looked sideways at Daddy. "That was a deep one!" I gasped, my teeth still rattling in my head.

"I told you to watch out," Momma said.

Daddy gave her a stern look. His face softened when his eyes shifted to me. I was still holding my hat on with both hands. Daddy grinned.

It was three miles from our farm to the church in Crossroads. Even for someone who had never driven the route before, they would know when they were leaving the valley and approaching Crossroads. It was like coming out of a tunnel. The dense forest along much of the way opened to a vast, rolling plain.

Crossing the river marked the end of the valley. From there, it was less than a half-mile to Crossroads proper. The church sat beside the schoolhouse and was just this side of the two dozen or so houses and businesses clustered around the intersection where the valley road met the highway.

We were always one of the first families to arrive for church. Momma and Daddy liked to get there early so they could talk with folks beforehand, catching up on the latest goings-on.

I was more interested in other things—like ringing the church bell. We kids were allowed to ring it every Sunday, as long as we took turns.

Today was my turn to ring the bell.

Bill went with Momma and Daddy to join the knot of people gathered in front of the church. Ed, Marty, and me raced around the corner and stomped up the stairs of the assembly hall, sounding like a herd of stampeding buffalo.

I got to the top first and pushed the heavy door open. The alcove of the bell tower was just inside. It smelled like Momma's mahogany hope chest.

Several kids who lived nearby were already there. Most of them showed up in case I was late, hoping they might be chosen to ring the bell instead.

I hung up my hat and sweater.

"Are you ready?" Ed asked.

I nodded.

Ed walked over and grabbed the bell rope from its hook on the wall. He was too big to ring the bell anymore, so Pastor Morton put him in charge of keeping the younger kids from getting too rambunctious when they rang it.

Ed took the responsibility seriously. He held the rope a

minute or so longer, waiting for the big hand and the second hand to meet on the twelve.

He was just about to hand me the rope when the back door of the assembly hall slammed shut, and somebody came slip-slapping up the back steps in what sounded like pajama sandals. "I'm here! I'm here! Don't give my turn away!" they shouted.

I knew the voice and recognized the towering figure as she appeared to rise out of the floor. She tripped over her dress at the top of the stairs, then threw back her head to get the hair out of her eyes. It was Mary Belle Baxter.

Mary Belle was a husky girl. She looked like a tall, burly boy in a dress and long, brown hair. Of course, nobody ever came right out and said that to her, not unless they wanted to get pounded.

Mary Belle and I were best friends once. She was a year older. We weren't exactly the perfect fit. It definitely wasn't the kind of friendship Momma had in mind when she told me to choose my friends wisely. But Mary Belle was the only girl close to my age for miles around.

Our friendship started to go haywire after Mary Belle's daddy got tired of the feast-or-famine life of a farmer. He sold their farm, bought the local gas station-repair shop, built a house, and moved the family to Crossroads.

Mary Belle and I stayed friends for a while longer, but eventually we grew apart. The distance wasn't the problem. It was Mary Belle. She thought she was the queen of Sheba or something because her family now had indoor plumbing, electricity, and fancy electric appliances.

We didn't have any of those things in the valley. Not yet, anyway.

Mary Belle started to think she was too good to be seen with valley folks. "Bumpkins," she called them. I suppose she didn't realize that included me.

Now we were anything but friends.

"Are you two going to stare at each other all day, or are you going to ring the bell, Ruby Mae?" Ed asked.

He rarely called me Ruby Mae. I took it as a sign of irritation. The second hand on the clock had already passed the twelve and ticked toward the three.

I nodded. "Sorry."

Ed held out the rope.

"Not so fast," Mary Belle said, grabbing it.

But Ed held fast. He glared at Mary Belle. "I think it's Ruby's turn," he said, growling low like a dog about to bite. He tugged on the rope but couldn't wrestle it from Mary Belle's grip.

"It's not her turn." Mary Belle gave the rope a jerk. She couldn't get it away from Ed, either. "It's my turn," she snarled.

I thought sure there was going to be a fight. Ed surprised me when he seemed to relax. A grin spread across his face.

"Okay. How we going to settle this?" he asked.

It was suddenly quiet. Then, Billy Hancock piped up: "Indian leg wrestling."

The boys around Billy chortled. The girls gasped, then giggled. I almost busted out laughing myself. No way was I going to Indian leg wrestle in a dress, not to mention doing it in church.

"Rock, paper, scissors," chimed in a meek, little voice. It was Sarah Burkhardt. She stood behind Billy. All I could see of Sarah was her head as she peeked around him.

Rock, paper, scissors was all the rage, ever since Judy Dickson read about it in an article about Japan and gave an oral report in front of the whole school.

Ed smiled. "Well?" he asked, looking first at me, then at Mary Belle.

"Suits me fine," Mary Belle said.

She was the last person I wanted to go up against. Mary Belle was good at the game. Real good. We had played it endlessly when we were friends. While other kids would fall for my tricks, Mary Belle had seen them all and was rarely fooled.

I nodded to Ed. "Okay. Let's play."

"Just don't you be cheating, Ruby Mae Ryan," Mary Belle growled.

An insult like that used to get me hopping mad. But I'd been working on taming my temper. Momma said it was unbecoming of a girl to go around blowing her top and kicking and biting other kids when they said something mean or rotten.

I just smiled. Beneath the smile, I was seething.

Mary Belle mocked me with her own fake smile, waggling her head back and forth as she stepped up and stood not more than six inches away.

Mary Belle was the tallest kid in school. On the other hand, I was the shortest in the upper grades. I might have been intimidated if I could have seen her scary face, but she stood so close all I could see was her nostrils when I looked up.

I felt the urge to punch her, but I settled for trying to push her away. She didn't budge.

Mary Belle smiled, then stepped back on her own accord.

"Ready?" she asked. She crouched low and raised her fist.

I got into position. "Ready."

It got so quiet you could have heard a hummingbird slurp.

"One! Two! Three!" Mary Belle and I counted in unison, pounding our fists into our open hands with each number.

"Paper!" I yelled. A fraction of a second later, I played my hand sign.

As I said, Mary Belle was good. The word "paper" registered with her instantly. I'm sure she thought I was pulling my usual trick, where I would play the opposite of what I shouted, which was rock. She played paper because it beats rock.

But I played scissors.

There we were, frozen for a moment. All eyes on us. My two fingers spread. Mary Belle's hand held flat.

"Scissors cut paper!" someone shouted. "Ruby wins!"

Mary Belle straightened with a jerk. "Cheater!" she yelled, slapping my hand away.

"Who you calling a cheater?" I demanded, lunging toward her. Ed grabbed one of my pigtails, and I stopped as suddenly as a mean dog at the end of its rope.

Mary Belle paid me no mind. She stomped across the floor, yanked open the heavy door like it was nothing, and slammed it shut behind her.

"Looks like somebody's a sore loser," Ed said. He motioned to Billy. "Give me a hand, will you?"

Ed and Billy stood on either side of me, and each grabbed an arm and a leg.

"Are you ready?"

"Uh-huh."

"One, two, three—lift!" Ed huffed.

They launched me into the air, and I grabbed the bell's rope as far up as possible.

"Okay! Let me go!" I said.

A second later, I dropped like a rock. Just before my tippy toes brushed the floor, the first clang of the bell sounded. The next moment I was jerked upward. When I reached the top, I was three or four feet above everybody else. The bell clanged again, and I dropped toward the floor.

It was like being on the end of a yo-yo string.

I must have gone up and down a dozen times or more. I stretched and pulled like pumping a swing, trying to gain height. It was so much fun I didn't want to stop.

"Wrap it up!" Ed shouted over the clanging of the bell.

"Just a few more," I pleaded as I came down face-to-face

with him. I was already headed up again before he answered.

"I don't think that's a good idea."

"Why not?"

Ed nodded toward the side entrance to the sanctuary. Pastor Morton stood there with his arms folded across his chest.

It was time for church.

Our family always sat together in the third pew on the right. All except Daddy this Sunday. He had snuck away after greeting folks. He sometimes spent Sunday mornings sitting on the porch of Mr. Abbott's store, drinking coffee and shooting the breeze with Mr. Abbott, Henry, and a few of the other regulars who gathered there.

On the other hand, Momma never missed a Sunday service. She loved everything about it, especially the sermons and singing hymns. She sang them loud and off-key. Just like me.

After singing, we children were excused to go to the basement for Bible classes. The adults stayed for Pastor Morton's sermon.

Momma had let me stay to listen to the sermon once. I fell asleep. Can't say that I've stayed since. Bible class was a lot more fun and interesting.

After today's class, me and Marty caught up with Momma in the sanctuary as she was getting ready to leave. The sermon must have been another snoozer. I noticed widow Murphy asleep in her pew.

"Wonderful sermon," Momma said as she shook the pastor's hand.

Pastor Morton liked to greet each of his parishioners as they left to go home. He even shook hands with us kids. I liked that about him.

"Thank you, Margaret," Pastor Morton said. "I hope to see James here next Sunday. We missed him last week, too, didn't we?"

"I'll tell him you noticed," Momma said.

Daddy was waiting for us in the truck.

"You missed a good sermon, James," Momma said as she passed his window.

Daddy got out and hustled to the other side of the truck to open the door for Momma and me.

"Sorry to hear that," Daddy said. "You'll have to tell me all about it on the way home."

The older boys came running and tumbled into the back. No doubt they had been up to mischief somewhere.

Often, I got to go over to my friend Virginia's house after church. Her family went to early Mass in Thackeray, so they were usually back before our church let out. Virginia would wait for me at the school playground to see if I could come over.

Not this Sunday. Not while I was grounded.

As our truck started slowly across the parking area, the school came into view. There was Virginia, sitting on a swing, watching for me to come out the back door of the church as I usually did.

"Virginia!" I yelled out Daddy's window.

Daddy frowned.

"Sorry, Daddy," I said, apologizing for yelling in his ear.

It was no use anyway. Virginia was too far away to hear me. I started to wave, trying to get her attention. I watched and waved all the way to the road, hoping she would look this way. She never did.

My nose was pressed against the back window as Daddy turned onto the valley road and drove off. I watched as Virginia disappeared in a cloud of dust.

Chapter 5

BEST MONDAY EVER

It felt wonderful to get out of the house again. Freedom could not have come on a prettier morning. It was clear and brisk, the sun peeking over the eastern ridge. Its rays poured into the valley like a bowl of golden punch.

Marty usually walked to school with me. Not today. I had to leave early, and he wasn't ready, so Momma said it was okay to go without him. Marty could ride into Crossroads with Daddy.

There was no time to dawdle, either. Virginia and I had flag duty this week. We were supposed to raise the flag before school started, then take it down and fold it after school.

I looked forward to the walk alone. I could go at my own pace. Besides, there wasn't a minute of peace or quiet when Marty was with me. His constant chatter scared away the wildlife and ruined the view.

I loved the texture and color of the fields and meadows woven together with those of the forest. Every now and again, I passed a farm, but mostly the valley was wild.

Where the woods skirted the road, the vegetation was thick and green. Salmonberry, ferns, blackberry vines, and a jumble of other plants created a nearly impassable barrier of underbrush. Yet animals had no trouble slipping through it without a trace, like ghosts walking through a wall.

My favorite wild thing—other than the animals—was the creek. It followed the road almost all the way to Crossroads. It started in the Coast Range and swelled as it swallowed trickles and smaller streams along its way to the river. You couldn't always see the creek from the road as it snaked through the woods and across fields, but you could always hear it. It was never far away.

Electric poles lined one side of the valley road. They stood straight and tall, like trees without limbs. Newly planted. Soon, they would have wires hanging from one to the next, all the way up the valley and beyond.

I liked to count the poles on my way to school. It made the three-mile walk seem shorter. The most I ever counted was eighty-three poles, but there were more than that between our farm and Crossroads. I would lose count because of my soft spot for animals, flowers, or passing automobiles. On that account, I always waved. It was the neighborly thing to do, whether you liked the folks or not.

Friendly dogs would come out to greet me, too. They knew I was good for a scratch behind the ears. But most dogs kept their distance and barked. They wanted passersby to know it was their territory.

One of those dogs was Buster. He had a ferocious bark, even though he mostly did it lying down. He started barking as soon as you passed one property line, and he didn't stop until you crossed the other. He wasn't mean, exactly, but he wasn't sociable either.

The farms disappeared altogether before you got to the river. They were replaced by a stretch of woods that swallowed the road and everything around it. On breezy days, the play between sun and trees created the most beautiful light show when sunbeams filtered through the trees and danced on the road to the rhythm of the wind.

At the far end of the woods was a halo of light where the road left the trees. When you reached it, you knew you were almost to Crossroads. It was just a short jog to the river, over the bridge, up a gentle rise, and then you were there.

Only the top of the schoolhouse and the church bell tower were visible from the bridge, but I could see everything by the time I crested the hill. As always, Virginia was there watching for me.

She launched herself out of the swing when I came into view. As she ran, her thick hair bounced from shoulder to shoulder. She looked like a twelve-year-old Dorothy Lamour, the movie star, with long dark hair, dark eyes, and a beautiful smile. It was easy to see why all the boys were sweet on her.

"What happened to you yesterday?" Virginia asked, shifting gears to a walk. She hooked her arm in mine, and we walked together the rest of the way.

"It's a long story."

"Give me the short version now and the long version at lunch."

"I'm grounded all week."

"Oh. I'm so sorry," Virginia said. "I was looking forward to having you show me how to catch crawfish in the river after school."

"Yeah, me too. Maybe you can spend the night next weekend when I'm ungrounded, and I can show you how to catch them in my creek."

Virginia rarely came to my house, and she had never stayed the night. "I can't," she said.

"How come?"

"Father is teaching a cooking class in Thackeray. He and the car will be gone all weekend."

"Ride your bicycle."

Virginia wrinkled her nose. She did that when she felt uncomfortable about something. I don't think she knew she was doing it.

"I don't know," she hedged.

"Why not?"

"It's an awful long way."

"You can always take breaks if you get tired."

"It's hard to ride a bike on gravel, you know, especially with so many potholes to dodge."

I could tell she was making excuses because she didn't want to venture that far from home on her own. For most people, it wouldn't be a big deal. It was for Virginia. She wasn't what you would call independent.

"Oh, come on," I said. "You can do it. Think of it as an adventure."

She sighed. "I'll think about it."

I'm pretty sure that meant no.

Virginia wasn't a fan of being outside. Not to mention, she always wore a dress, even when playing outdoors. Not me. Outdoors wasn't much fun in a dress.

"How's your fundraising coming along for the you-know-what?" Virginia asked, changing the subject.

"It could be better. I'm still seventeen dollars and eleven cents short."

"That reminds me. Mother turns forty on Friday. Father wants to make crawfish etouffee for her birthday supper."

"Ate-two, what?"

"No. Etouffee," Virginia repeated, giggling. "It's like a thick, spicy gumbo."

"How many crawdads does your daddy need?"

"Four dozen."

"Sure that's enough?"

"Yeah. It's just for mother and father. Emeline and I don't like crawfish."

"Okay. I'll bring them Friday."

"Perfect."

"I can't go to the restaurant on account of being grounded, so I'll give them to you before school."

"Father asked me to say 'thank you,' especially for doing it on such short notice."

"He's always welcome. Got to take care of my best customer."

"Cha-ching!" Virginia said. "Forty-eight cents more for your money jar."

"Yeah, but I've still got a long way to go." I shook my head. "Being grounded a week doesn't help. There's got to be a way to make more money, even while cooped up in my room."

"Seems to me you're already making money every which way you can. You must be the richest girl in the valley."

"Maybe so, but none of the jobs are steady."

"Let's see, there's crawfish catching. Washing Friday-night dishes for father. Helping Mr. Abbott deliver ice on Tuesday afternoons. That's three. What else?"

"Sometimes I babysit, or watch and feed livestock for folks when they're away." I stopped to think. "And I write out invitations and such for special occasions. Mrs. Prescott says I have the prettiest handwriting."

"That's four, five, and six. Anything else?"

I shook my head. "See, that's all there is."

"Sounds like a lot to me."

"But it's not enough, I tell you. I need to raise the money before we get electricity. That gives me only another two or three months."

Virginia put her hand on my shoulder. "I'm sure you'll figure something out. You always do."

Chapter 6

THE NEW BOY

At lunch, I told Virginia about the bobcat, how Marty tricked me, and everything else. I thought she was going to cry when I got to the part about Momma's vase. Virginia was like that, always feeling other people's pain.

"How did your mother take it?"

"She was livid."

"Lots of yelling, huh?" Virginia cringed.

"Actually, no. Momma hardly said a word."

"That's a good thing, isn't it?"

"Not so much. Momma's only like that when she's really mad. She was on the verge of tears and probably too choked up to say anything."

"Oh. I'm so sorry."

I shook my head. It hurt to think about it, even now.

"My mother would have skinned me alive if I'd have brought a wild animal in the house."

"You don't think extra chores and being grounded is enough punishment?"

"Oh, no. No. That's not what I meant," Virginia said. "It's just it could have been worse. You could have been grounded for a lot longer."

Leave it to Virginia to look on the bright side.

It sure felt good to talk with someone, even if I didn't like the topic. I'd been going stir-crazy at home. With Virginia, I could talk about anything.

"Hey, look," Virginia said. "There's that new boy."

"What new boy?" I asked, looking up from my half-peeled orange.

"Over there."

"Oh, *that* new boy." I'd seen Mrs. Prescott showing him around the school on Friday afternoon.

He was a farm boy, not from Crossroads. You could tell by the way he dressed. His blue jeans folded up at the ankles and Western shirt were two clues. The hanky peeking out of his back pocket was another. The dead giveaway was his worn, dirty work boots.

Virginia nudged my elbow. "Stop staring," she said, looking the other way. I think she wanted me to do the same, but I didn't.

I admit it, I was staring. But I didn't mean anything by it. It was curiosity, that's all. Not only was the boy new, but he looked the part. Alone. Uneasy. Out of place.

He slowly wandered the schoolyard, sneaking looks at the pairs and groups of kids sitting together eating lunches. He must have hoped someone would notice and give him an excuse to strike up a conversation.

"Paul Johnson," Virginia said, interrupting my thoughts.

"What?"

"That's the new boy's name. Paul Johnson. He's thirteen."

Virginia made it her business to know everybody and their family history. I didn't care for nosy people and their gossip. It was one of the things I overlooked about Virginia.

"Uh-huh. I saw him last week." I was ready to move on to another topic of conversation.

Apparently, Virginia wasn't.

"Me, too," she said. "His parents bought Mary Belle's old farm. They're going to raise sheep. I don't know what that takes, but it's a smelly business, for sure."

"Better than goats."

"Maybe so, but I'm glad father is in the restaurant business."

That's another thing I overlooked about Virginia. She was a city girl and didn't know much about life in the country and sometimes said hurtful things. Not on purpose, mind you. She just didn't know any better.

Virginia moved to Crossroads two years ago. She had spent most of her life in New Orleans. In places like that, you didn't need to know a lick about cows or sheep or plowing or milking, or anything else about country life.

Of course, just as I overlooked Virginia's flaws, I was sure there were things she overlooked about me, too. Like my temper.

Virginia sat up suddenly. "Now, that's interesting!" she said.

"What?"

"Look over there." Virginia nodded toward Paul.

Mary Belle had struck up a conversation with him. As usual, she was doing all the talking. He just stood there grinning, trying to figure out what to do with his hands as Mary Belle jabbered on.

Virginia studied the scene a moment. "It's obvious she likes him," she said.

I looked closer. What did Virginia see that I didn't?

Mary Belle's ears must have been burning because she turned and looked right at us. Her manner changed in an instant. She appeared to calm down and moved more slowly, gesturing gracefully with her hands as she talked.

Then Mary Belle did something I never expected: She grabbed Paul's hand and began leading him around the schoolyard. As they walked, holding hands, Mary Belle pointed out various things and hollered to kids and waved as if she was some kind of big shot.

Paul may have been looking for a friend, but probably not one quite like Mary Belle.

"Looks like she's giving him the grand tour," I said, still a bit surprised. I had known Mary Belle my whole life. I'd never known her to be forward like that. She must have really liked the boy.

"He doesn't like her," Virginia said, shaking her head. She folded her arms. "He's just being nice."

I gave Virginia a puzzled look. "How do you know stuff like that?"

"Oh, I can tell," she said, not taking her eyes off Mary Belle and her new friend.

What happened next almost made me squirt juice out of my nose. While Paul was looking the other way, Mary Belle whipped her head around and stuck out her tongue. Two seconds later, she was back to jawing with him as if nothing had happened.

"Did you see that?" Virginia gasped. "How rude! She stuck her tongue out at me."

"I don't think so."

"She most certainly did."

"No, I mean, I don't think she was sticking it out at you," I explained. "She probably meant it for me. I'm the one who beat her at rock, paper, scissors yesterday."

"Either way, it's rude!"

"That's Mary Belle. Seems there's no love lost between her and me."

"I can see why," Virginia huffed. She started to put things away to calm herself—first her leftovers and then the empty milk bottle. She folded her napkin perfectly, placed it on top of everything else, and buckled her basket closed. "Are you ready to go back in?"

"I suppose," I said. "The bell will be ringing any minute now."

I took one last look around the schoolyard. Mary Belle and Paul were nowhere in sight. By now, he was probably hiding from her in the boys' bathroom or the library, and she was off telling friends tall tales about how much Paul liked her.

As Virginia and I walked up the steps, I thought again about how good it felt to be out of the house. Lunchtime with Virginia was the longest I'd spent talking to anyone since being grounded. It was the highlight of my day and would be the highlight every day until this weekend when I was finally ungrounded.

Chapter 7

EVERYONE CAN PLAY A PART

It was hard to believe Saturday was finally here. After a week of being stuck in the house and doing every chore Momma could think of, I would be ungrounded in just a few hours. All I had to do was finish loading the lemonade wagon and take it up the road to where Daddy and the rest of the crew were putting up electric poles, and then I'd be free. Or so I thought.

My hopes sank when Virginia suddenly appeared on her bicycle. She turned into our drive, waving and ringing the bell on her handlebars as she rode.

I was certain Momma would consider this a breach of my grounding. A sense of doom came over me. I started running toward Virginia. I had to stop her before Momma heard that darn bell.

"Hey, Ruby!" Virginia said as her bicycle slid to a stop. "Bet you're surprised to see me."

"If you only knew," I groaned.

Virginia's smile faded. "What?" she asked. "You don't look too happy."

"Of course, I'm happy to see you, Virginia. I'm always glad to see you."

"Then, what?" she asked, lowering the kickstand on her bicycle.

"Momma might not be so glad."

She put her hands on her hips. "I thought your mother liked me."

"She does. It's just that I'm not ungrounded until this afternoon."

Virginia gasped. "Say no more." She jumped back on her bicycle.

"Wait!"

"I don't want to get you in trouble," she said. "I don't think I could stand it if you were grounded another week!"

Just then, the porch screen door slapped shut, and Momma walked down the back steps. She eyed the wagon parked where I had left it, then looked around. That's when she spotted me—and Virginia.

I held my breath as Momma walked toward us.

"Hello, Virginia," she said in her sweet, company voice. "What brings you all the way out here?"

"Hello, Mrs. Ryan. I came to visit Ruby."

I just had to say something. "Momma, she didn't know," I exclaimed.

"Know what, honey?"

"She didn't know I was still grounded."

Virginia shook her head and started talking fast. "No, ma'am, I didn't know. I'm sorry. Truly I am. I would never do anything to disobey you or get Ruby into trouble."

Momma got one of those looks, the kind where you could tell she was trying not to smile. "No, I don't suppose you would."

"No, ma'am," Virginia said for good measure.

"Ruby could probably use a hand with the lemonade run. Would you like to help?"

"Sure. I guess."

"Are you certain it's all right, Momma?" I asked. She was usually strict about groundings and such, so I was surprised when she offered to let Virginia come along.

"Of course," she said, turning and heading back to the house. "But you better get moving before I change my mind."

"Yes, Momma."

She didn't have to tell me twice.

"Come on," I said to Virginia, "you can help me finish loading the wagon."

We went to the kitchen to get glasses, a ladle, a sponge, and dishtowels. We packed them in a box and stowed it in the wagon, which was already loaded with a milk can half-full of lemonade and two buckets of water for washing and rinsing glasses. All the containers had lids to keep them from spilling. I added a chunk of ice to the lemonade before we left.

"Are you ready?" I asked.

Virginia nodded. "Now, mush!" she said, snapping her arm forward as if she had a whip.

I pulled, she pushed. The wagon crunched up the gravel drive and onto the valley road.

"I'll bet you didn't know that's the farthest I've ever ridden my bicycle."

That didn't surprise me. Virginia's parents were overprotective, especially her momma.

"I'm proud of you, Virginia. How did you get your momma to let you go?"

"Oh, I didn't ask her. I asked father before he left for class."

I grinned.

"You know, when we're done with the lemonade run, this might be the farthest you've ever walked, too," I said. "Not bad. Two firsts in one day."

"How far is it?"

"About two miles roundtrip. Maybe a little more."

"Oh." She didn't sound too excited. "Oh, okay."

"Don't worry. If you get tired, I can give you a ride back in the wagon."

The wagon seemed light when we started, but it got heavier the farther we went. The loose gravel and potholes made it slow going. It didn't help that we were going uphill most of the way.

"I'm glad I didn't do this by myself."

Virginia laughed. "You can say that again. By the way, where exactly are we going?"

"Up there," I said, pointing to the low rise in front of us. "Probably another half-mile beyond the top there."

"What's your father doing way out here?"

"Putting up electric poles."

"Why's he doing that?"

"Somebody's got to."

"No, I mean, why doesn't the power company have their people do it?"

"He *is* their people," I said, stopping. I dropped the wagon handle to give my arm a rest.

"Your father works for the power company?"

"Not exactly," I said. "Daddy's helping the electric cooperative."

"What's that?"

"It's a new kind of power company. Daddy and other folks in the valley started it."

"What for? There's already a power company, the one where father buys our electricity."

"Sure, but that one didn't want to bring electricity to the valley. They said it wasn't worth it, which is why the power line only goes as far as Crossroads and stops."

"I didn't know that."

"Yup. Almost everybody in the valley has joined the electric co-op. We're going to build our own power line, just like other folks are doing, all around the country."

"Sounds like you know a lot about it."

"Not really. I just hear Daddy talk." I picked up the wagon handle. "You ready to go again?"

Virginia nodded. "But how 'bout we change places. I don't like all the dust back here."

It was amusing to watch Virginia pull the wagon. She went out of her way to avoid every pothole and puddle. We weaved all over the road.

"So, how much you getting paid for this?" Virginia asked.

"Nothing."

She looked over her shoulder. "Really? I'd think this would be worth something."

"Oh, it is. But some things you don't do for money."

"Yeah, but this is a lot of work."

"I know. But like Daddy says, if the valley's going to get electricity, everybody's got to pitch in and help," I said. "This is me doing my part."

"Seems like an awful lot of fuss just for electricity."

I stopped pushing, and the wagon came to a dead stop.

"Hey!" Virginia exclaimed, dropping the handle and turning around.

"A fuss? That's easy for you to say," I said, trying not to sound mean. "You already have electricity and don't know what it's like without it."

Virginia shrugged. "I suppose that's true. Unless you count when the electricity went out in a hurricane," Virginia said, referring to when she lived in Louisiana. She had told me all kinds of scary stories about hurricanes.

"Well, I've never had electricity. Ever."

Virginia picked up the wagon handle, signaling she was ready to move on.

"I guess you're right. It would be hard without electricity," she said. "I can't imagine life without a fridge."

"No electric lights, either," I chimed in.

"No electric radio or stove or iron," she added.

"No indoor plumbing."

Virginia's head spun around so fast she almost stumbled. "I didn't know you needed electricity for that," she gasped, blushing.

"Sure, you do. At least that's what Daddy says. Something about electricity powering pumps to bring water in and then move everything out after you flush."

"That's too much information for me, thank you very much."

I chuckled. Why didn't that surprise me?

When we got to the top of the hill, we could see the men working up ahead. Some dug holes, while others set electric poles in the holes.

Daddy and four other men were wrestling a pole into place when we rolled up. They lifted it using just their hands and brute strength. When it was too high to reach with their hands, they used long, skinny rods to continue pushing up the pole. Every now and then, another fella used an X-shaped device to hold the pole in place while the other men shifted positions and continued lifting.

Another crew of men was doing the same thing farther up the road, and beyond them were three pairs of men digging more holes. One of the pairs was Bill and Ed.

A skinny fella in a white shirt, tie, and glasses watched the men as they worked. He must have been the boss. He was the only one not wearing work gloves.

Me and Virginia didn't want to get in the way, so we sat on the wagon and watched a while.

Once a pole was in the ground, two men held it straight

while the others shoveled gravel and soil around it. When the hole was heaping full, they used metal bars and sledgehammers to tamp down the dirt. They filled and tamped until the ground around the pole held it firmly in place.

"Let's take a break," the boss man said to the men nearby. Then he whistled and yelled at the workers up the road. "Break time!"

The men lined up for lemonade. They were sweaty, dirty, and thirsty.

Virginia wiped the dust off the glasses, while I filled them and passed out the lemonade. Most of the men said, "Thank you," and tipped their hats to show appreciation.

"Ruby!" Daddy called, mothing me to go to him. "Hey, Ruby! Over here!"

I filled a glass for Daddy.

"Here, take this," I said, handing Virginia the ladle. "I gotta go."

"But …"

"Don't worry. I shouldn't be gone long," I said. "Remember, only one glass each until everyone has some. Then they can have seconds and thirds."

I hated to desert Virginia like that, but Daddy needed me. It had to be something important for him to call me away from my work.

"Hi, Daddy."

"Hey, Sugar."

Daddy and I walked to where the next pole was ready to be raised. We sat down on a moss-covered rock, and Daddy drank his lemonade. He sipped it slow to make the cold, tart goodness last.

"I've got some good news," Daddy said between sips. "You see Mr. Flanagan over there?"

He was standing in line for lemonade.

"Yes, sir," I said, making a sour face. "The old crank."

"Ruby!" he growled, more surprised than angry.

"I'm sorry, Daddy. But it's true. Mr. Flanagan hates girls. He never smiles, and I don't like how he always calls me Red."

"I understand. Mr. Flanagan can be difficult sometimes, but that's no excuse to be disrespectful."

Difficult? I could think of better words than that to describe Mr. Flanagan.

"I'm sorry, Daddy," I said, more interested in moving on to the next subject than the apology itself. "So, what about Mr. Flanagan?"

"While he and I were talking, the conversation turned to strawberries. I asked him about letting you pick this season."

That got my attention. A body can make a lot of money picking strawberries. I wanted to pick last year, but Mr. Flanagan wouldn't let me.

"What did he say?"

Daddy didn't answer. Instead, he drank the last of his lemonade.

The suspense was unbearable. "Well?" I asked.

Daddy smiled. "He said yes."

"For real?"

Daddy nodded, smiling wider. "How 'bout that?"

"That's great!" I yelped, suddenly feeling bad for calling Mr. Flanagan a crank. "When do I start?"

"Memorial Day."

"Wow! That's the end of next week."

"Uh-huh. It's a little earlier than usual. With all the good weather, the berries are coming on fast."

"I'll be ready!" I gave him a hug. "Thank you, Daddy."

"You're welcome," he said, handing me his empty glass. "Now, why don't you head on back. It looks like Virginia's had about enough lemonade duty."

My feet had wings as I ran to share the good news.

Most of the men were back at work, so Virginia had taken everything out of the wagon and was lying down in it.

"Guess what!" I said, out of breath.

"Where've you been?" she asked, without budging.

"I'm going to be rich."

Virginia sat up. "I beg your pardon?"

"Okay. Maybe not rich, but for sure I'll be able to earn enough to buy my secret surprise. Isn't that wonderful?"

Virginia gasped. "How will you make that much money?" she asked. She slid over to make room for me to sit down.

"Daddy got me a job."

"Where?"

"Picking berries for Mr. Flanagan."

"You mean grumpy old Mr. Flanagan? The man who eats half his order at the restaurant then sends it back because he says it's cold or undercooked? That Mr. Flanagan?"

"Yup."

"I can't believe you'd do that."

"What? It makes no difference if he's nice or grumpy. It's cash money, all the same."

"No, I mean, I can't believe you're going to get down in the dirt and pick strawberries."

"What's wrong with that?"

"You'll ruin your clothes, for one thing. And, besides, it isn't ladylike."

Virginia constantly worried about things like that.

"Well, if I ruin my clothes, I'll buy new ones. I'm going to be rich, after all."

"Very funny," she said. "Are there any other girls?"

"No, just me. Mr. Flanagan doesn't usually allow girls. He says a berry field is no place for them."

"For once, I agree with Mr. Flanagan."

I stood up and brushed off the seat of my overalls. "Well, Mr. Flanagan is the one who hired me, and since you agree with him, it must mean you think that's okay too."

"Touché!"

"How about we head home? I can't wait to tell Momma the good news."

"Suits me fine."

Before we left, Virginia and I drank the last of the lemonade. It was extra tart because everything had settled to the bottom. Then we washed out the glasses, dumped and stacked the buckets, and put everything back into the wagon.

The wagon was much lighter—that is, until Virginia sat down in it.

"What are you doing?" I asked.

"I'm tired, Ruby," she whined. "Plus, you did say something about giving me a ride back. I know you were only joking, but please? Pretty please?"

I grinned. "Oh, all right."

"Thanks. You're a gem, Ruby."

"You're welcome. Besides, you've got to save your strength for the three-mile bicycle ride back to Crossroads," I teased.

Virginia groaned.

Chapter 8

A LOCAL LEGEND

It felt good to be ungrounded. I wasted no time taking advantage of my newfound freedom and got permission to go to Virginia's house after school.

But first, she had a piano lesson. I could have stayed to listen, but I chose not to because Virginia wasn't much of a piano player.

I'd much rather hang out with Henry if he was around or go down to the river and practice skipping rocks until Virginia finished her lesson.

Henry wasn't hard to find. He sat out front of Mr. Abbott's store most afternoons unless fish were biting.

His favorite chair was the one on the end closest to the door, next to the newspaper box. It was a sturdy captain's chair with armrests and a padded seat. Everybody knew that was Henry's spot. He could sit there for hours chewing the fat with anyone who would listen.

When I strolled up, Henry was standing over the paper box scanning the Thackeray newspaper's latest edition, sipping a cherry cola.

I slumped into the chair next to his.

"What's the occasion?" I asked, eyeing Henry as he read the paper on top of the pile.

"Howdy-do, Ruby," he said, distracted, still reading.

"Hi, Henry."

He turned and patted my shoulder. "Good to see you, youngster. Now, what's that you say?"

"What are you all dressed up for?"

"Oh, that," he said, admiring his clothes. "I do look pretty sharp today, don't I?"

"Sure do."

I was used to seeing Henry dressed in worn and faded work clothes, a rope for a belt, and boots with all the color scuffed off.

Not today.

Henry wore a white shirt and a narrow black tie. A belt with a fancy silver buckle held up blue dungarees that looked brand new. They were tucked into the tops of his cowboy boots, black as stovepipes and polished to a glossy shine.

The only Henry I recognized stuck out above the too-tight shirt collar, his face the color and texture of wrinkled cedar bark, dark eyes, bushy gray eyebrows. He had an odd, misshapen nose and ears with gray hair sprouting from the lobes. As always, he wore his tattered, sweat-stained fishing hat.

The way he looked reminded me of when Ed and I put Ed's Sunday school jacket and tie on Wanda, our goat, for Halloween. The jacket and tie were spiffy, but Wanda definitely looked out of place.

"I'm going to Thackeray with Ma," he said as he sat down beside me. He started to chuckle. "She's driving herself around the country. Never driven a car before. Says she wants to see the sights before she's too old."

I cocked my head and looked at him funny.

Henry was old enough to be my grandfather. I never

considered his momma might still be alive. She would have to be like a hundred years old.

"Are you pulling my leg?" I asked.

"Would I do that?"

I nodded. "Uh-huh."

He grinned, his upper lip glistening with sweat. "I suppose I deserve that," he said, chuckling. "But, nah, this time it's for true. Cross my heart." He drew an X across his chest with a gnarled finger.

"When's your momma going to be here?"

"Anytime now."

I folded my arms across my chest. "Think I'll wait with you, then."

Henry smiled and looked up the empty highway. He took off his hat, licked his fingers, and tried to tame a stand of wild, jet-black hairs. Beats me why they were sticking up. He had enough hair pomade to grease a wheel.

Henry had been a part of my life for as long as I could remember. He was the only adult I was allowed to call by his first name.

Grandpa and Henry spent so much time together that I thought they were brothers. Even after Grandpa passed away, I considered Henry family, and I think the feeling was mutual.

"You're here early," I said.

"Caught my limit."

"That was fast."

"Yes sirree, the fish were biting like a swarm of hungry mosquitoes," Henry said, scratching his chin. "Must be a surge in the mayfly hatch. Funny thing, I wasn't even using flies."

Henry was a fishing legend in these parts. Some considered him the world's greatest fisherman. Just ask him.

"You're lucky that way," I said, grinning, knowing my little prod would get a reaction out of him.

"Lucky? Puh!" he scoffed, pretending to be offended. He spat for dramatic effect.

Usually, Henry was a pretty good spitter, but a gust from a passing car caught the spitball and pushed it back toward us. It landed on the toe of one of his shiny boots.

I knew better than to laugh.

Henry cringed.

"You still have those flies I tied for you a while back?" he asked, trying to ignore the spit on his boot.

"I sure do."

"One of them is a mayfly. Perfect conditions to use it," Henry said. "You know what a mayfly looks like, don't you?"

"Course I do," I squawked, my head whipping around before I realized he was funning me back.

Henry was grinning. He liked to tease. That, and tell whoppers.

"Those brothers of yours would be mighty jealous if you came home with a stringer full of rainbows. Best place on the creek is the hole right there at your place, by the old mill."

"Thanks for the tip."

People came from all around to get Henry's fishing advice. A fortunate few spent a day fishing with him. Just as Daddy knew everything about fixing things, Henry knew everything about fishing—and a whole lot more.

He owned a shack along the river and mostly lived off the land. He didn't see much cash money. None of us did. But Henry took special pride in knowing he didn't need it. He figured he could always repurpose castoffs, trade with folks, and make, gather, or grow anything else he needed.

A big truck whooshed by the store. Henry's tie flew up and over his shoulder, and a cloud of dust swirled around us.

Henry readjusted his tie and smoothed it over his potbelly. "How's crawdad catching these days?"

"Good."

"You still saving your money for something special?"

"Uh-huh."

"For a new bicycle?"

"Nope."

"Your very own radio?"

"Nope."

"A canoe?"

"Nah," I said, giggling.

"I don't know. A canoe would come in mighty handy for catching crawdads. Or fishing."

"I suppose it would."

"So, aren't you going to tell me?"

I thought about it for a second. "I don't think so. But you can see it after I buy it."

"Oh. I see. A secret too big to tell old Henry, eh?" He took a drink of his cherry cola, pretending not to care.

We sat a while without talking.

"I ever tell you about Crawdad Haven?" Henry asked, the question coming out of nowhere.

I shook my head. "Not that I remember."

"Oh, you'd remember," he said, "especially you being the Crawdad Champ."

Henry had called me that ever since he taught me to catch crawdads, and I beat him in a contest to see who could catch the most. I'm pretty sure he let me win.

"What's Crawdad Haven?"

Henry's eyes got big around. He leaned toward me and whispered, "It's a place where hundreds—no, thousands—of crawdads gather together, just ripe for the pickings, for anyone who has a mind to catch 'em."

I folded my arms and gave Henry a sideways look. "Sounds pretty far-fetched to me."

"Puh!" he grunted, swatting away my opinion with a motion of his hand. "Suit yourself. I was going to tell you all about it, but maybe another time."

Henry finished his cherry cola.

Right about then, an automobile appeared up the highway. Henry and I watched it. To my way of thinking, it seemed different than the others that passed. It approached much more slowly and moved herky-jerky all over its side of the highway.

When it was still more than a quarter-mile off, the automobile started to ease into the gravel along the highway, creating a rooster tail of dust. Half a minute passed before it finally closed the distance with Mr. Abbott's store.

"This must be my ride," Henry said. He stood up, hiked his pants, and smoothed his tie again.

"Your momma?"

Henry nodded. "Here, take this," he said, sneaking the empty cola bottle to me.

"What's this for?"

"Ma doesn't like me drinking that stuff. Bad for the teeth," he said, smiling sheepishly. "Keep the two-cent return."

"Thanks, Henry."

The automobile crawled to a stop in front of the porch, the trailing cloud of dust passing it by and settling on everything in its path. It was a big, beautiful, burgundy-colored car with lots of chrome and headlights the size of dinner plates.

"Well, don't you look nice, Henry!" hollered the woman behind the steering wheel.

I couldn't see her, on account of the dust, but I could hear her plain as day.

"Hi, Ma!" Henry opened the car door and got in.

I followed him and looked in the window while he got settled. He leaned over and gave his momma a peck on the cheek. "Thanks for picking me up."

My eyes must have been open as wide as my mouth. I didn't believe Henry before, but now I did. The resemblance was unmistakable.

The woman looked just like I thought she would look at one hundred. She was a big woman, with more wrinkles and valleys on her face and neck than I'd ever seen before. Her hair was white and swirled in a bun, with a tiny, frilly hat pinned on top.

"Ma, this is Ruby Ryan," Henry said, turning to me. He grinned when he saw my face.

"What's wrong with her mouth?"

It was still wide-open. I snapped it shut.

"Nothing, Ma. She's just surprised to see you."

"Well, nice to meet you, Ruby Ryan."

"Nice to meet you, too, Mrs. ..., ah ..." I realized I didn't know Henry's last name.

"Pearl. You can call me Pearl."

I nodded, too embarrassed to call her by her first name. Kids just didn't do that. Unless, of course, it was Henry.

He still had a grin on his face. He put his elbow out the window and leaned toward me. "I never said I was pulling your leg."

I smiled, blushing.

"Now, if I could get another favor from you," said Henry.

"Sure. Name it."

Henry fished in his pocket and handed me a nickel. "Run this into Mr. Abbott for me, would you? It's for the newspaper."

"Why? You didn't take a paper."

"I got what I wanted from the newspaper," he said. "The nickel is for the news, not the paper. Now, will you do that for me?"

"If you say so."

"Good girl," he said, patting my arm.

I stepped back from the car as Henry's momma ground the gears and prepared to put the vehicle in motion.

"So long, Sugar," his momma said as the car slowly pulled away.

"Bye!" I waved.

Henry raised his hand and gave me a long, slow wave goodbye.

I couldn't help but laugh. At the rate the car was moving, it would probably take an hour to drive the fifteen miles to Thackeray.

Chapter 9

LAST-DAY TRADITIONS

The last week of school always tried my patience. This year was even worse since I was anxious to get on with summer vacation and start my new job. I thought the week might never end. But there we were, finally, the last hour of the last day of sixth grade.

All but two of the end-of-school traditions had been completed. Textbooks had been put away, and we had washed the floors, windows, chalkboards, and desktops. After that, we played games outside with the other classes and then wolfed down cupcakes and punch.

The only traditions left were cleaning out our desks and waiting to see who would get pranked.

Everyone was restless to leave. You could tell by the noise. Miss Radigan was out of the room for a few minutes and had left Devon Marshall in charge. He was the biggest, smartest kid in class. I'm not sure which of those traits most qualified him, but there he was, sitting behind Miss Radigan's desk like a big shot.

The rest of us were clustered around the room in small groups. Some chatted like magpies, while others played games to pass the time. Virginia and I sat on the shiny-clean floor playing jacks with two other girls. We were too busy to notice when Miss Radigan came back.

"Class," Miss Radigan said, trying not to yell. When that didn't work, she tried again, louder. "Hello? Class!" she shouted above the noise. "Please return to your seats. The sooner you get there, the sooner we can all leave."

Everybody stampeded back to their desks, and the room got quiet.

"The last thing I'd like you to do is clean out your desks. Take home anything that's yours, return school property to me, and wash out the inside of your desk," she said. "You may begin."

It got noisy again. Everyone wanted to finish as quickly as possible. We knew no one was going home until the last desk was clean. Even Miss Radigan was busy cleaning her desk.

Everything was going just dandy until someone let out an indescribable, ear-piercing shriek.

We all stopped to see who it was.

It was Miss Radigan. Her eyes bugged out and her mouth was open so wide we could see her fillings.

When she finally regained her composure, she said, "I see I have a mouse in my drawer." Her voice was an octave higher than usual.

Some kids gasped. Most tried not to bust out laughing, but a few couldn't help but titter.

"Silence, please," she said.

It got deathly quiet.

She glared at Devon. "You were sitting at my desk. Do you know anything about this?"

"Na, no, ma'am," he stuttered.

Miss Radigan scanned the other faces around the room.

"I would like the person who left me this ... this gift ... to please come up and remove it from my drawer."

Nobody got up.

"I'm waiting," Miss Radigan said sternly.

Still, nobody moved.

"Perhaps, I didn't make myself clear. Until the person responsible for putting this mouse in my desk reveals himself—or herself—no one has permission to leave. You will all remain at your desks until kingdom come."

The tension had gotten so bad I felt I had to do something. I raised my hand. Almost instantly, I regretted it.

"Ruby?" There was a look of shock on Miss Radigan's face. I realized she thought I was confessing. "Oh, no, ma'am. I didn't do it."

"Then why did you raise your hand?"

"I was volunteering to take the mouse out of your drawer."

"Do you know who did do this?"

"No, ma'am."

She studied me so hard I thought she was looking right through me.

"I'm just trying to be helpful, that's all," I said.

Finally, she nodded her head. "All right, you may remove the mouse. Are you sure you can do it without getting bitten or scratched?"

"Pretty sure," I said, walking to the front of the classroom. I had caught lots of mice.

"The bottom drawer," Miss Radigan said, pointing. She backed away, and I don't think it was just to give me more space to work.

I opened the drawer slowly. Sure enough, there was a small, brown ball of fur doing slow laps around the inside of the drawer. It was just a baby. As it turned a corner and presented its backside to me, I snatched it by the tail.

"Got your mouse," I said, holding it out to Miss Radigan.

"Ew! Take it outside, please," she said, cringing. She motioned me away.

I let the mouse go in the stand of trees between the school and the church. I figured that way a hawk wouldn't get it right off.

On my way back, the school doors swung open, and the first and second graders and the seventh and eighth graders came gushing out. They poured down the steps like water cascading over a rocky waterfall.

Paul Johnson was a seventh grader, but he had stayed behind for some reason. He was standing alone in the hallway when I walked in.

"Hi, Ruby."

I was dumbstruck. How did he know my name?

"Uh, hey there," I said.

I don't know why I stopped, but I did, even though I knew Miss Radigan was waiting for me and wouldn't dismiss class until I got back.

"My name's Paul."

"Yeah, I know. I mean, that's what I heard."

"What did you think of our little prank?"

"What prank?"

Paul frowned. "Come on. You really don't know?"

Then it hit me. "So, you're the one who put the mouse in Miss Radigan's desk."

"Uh-huh," he said, grinning. "We put one in all of the teachers' desks."

"That must have been some trick."

"Yup. We did it when everybody was outside playing games."

"My teacher screamed," I said.

"I know." The grin widened across Paul's face. "The whole school heard her."

"How did your teacher react?"

"Didn't say a word," he said, shaking his head. "She just scooped up the mouse and took it outside. Nobody but me and a couple other boys knew what she found."

"That takes all the fun out of it."

"You can say that again. But your teacher's reaction. Wow! That made up for it."

"You know you could get in a lot of trouble if they find out. Miss Radigan is pretty mad."

Paul's grin disappeared. "You won't tell, will you?"

"Of course not. I'm no tattletale."

"Thanks." He looked relieved. "Besides, if I get in trouble, my accomplices will too."

"What accomplices?"

"Your brother, for one."

Why wasn't I surprised?

Just then, the door of Marty's classroom opened, and he filed out with the rest of his class. He came over and stood between Paul and me.

"You ready to go?" Marty asked.

"No," I said. "My class hasn't been excused yet."

Marty looked at me like I was daft. "Not you, Ruby. Him," he said, pointing at Paul.

"Sure, I'm ready," Paul said. He turned and winked at me. "You're a good egg, Ruby. Thanks for keeping our little secret. See you around."

Then, he punched me in the shoulder. It was one of those punches where the knuckle hits the funny bone and it hurts. I couldn't believe it! I was just about to slug him back when Mrs. Prescott came out of the classroom and nearly bumped into us.

"Oh, hello, children," she said.

"Hello, Mrs. Prescott. Goodbye, Mrs. Prescott." Marty rattled as he made a beeline for the door.

"We were just leaving," Paul explained, walking backward toward Marty. "Goodbye, Mrs. Prescott. Have a good summer."

He and Marty were out the door in a flash. Their sudden departure didn't faze Mrs. Prescott. Teachers must get used to such guilty behavior.

"So, how about you, Ruby? Got anything exciting planned for summer?"

"Picking strawberries."

"How nice," she said, smiling. "I'll see you there."

"Really?" I couldn't believe my ears. Why would Mrs. Prescott pick strawberries? Everybody knew she didn't need money. She lived in the big house on the hill, on the other side of the river. It was a mansion compared to anything else around here. Why would she pick berries?

"Yes, really," she said. "You might say, I'm Mr. Flanagan's partner. He had the land and the know-how, but he needed somebody to help fund the endeavor, so I offered my assistance."

"Oh. I see."

I guess that meant I was working for Mr. Flanagan *and* Mrs. Prescott. I would really have to mind my p's and q's if I was going to survive strawberry season.

Chapter 10

UP BEFORE THE ROOSTER

Nothing wakes a body up like an early morning drive to pay respects to the dead.

It was Memorial Day, and we were on our way to the valley cemetery. I was wedged between Daddy and Momma. The boys were in the back of the truck, huddled under the blanket Daddy kept behind the seat for just such occasions.

The morning sky was still dark. Only a faint orange glow outlined the eastern ridge as we pulled up to the cemetery gate.

The sputter-wheeze of the engine shutting off scattered a bevy of quail and spooked two deer feeding on the long grass. The deer bounded away, dodging headstones as they went, and easily jumped the cemetery's four-foot stone wall and disappeared into the surrounding woods.

It was amazing how the grace and beauty of wild things made you stop and marvel. But there was no time to gawk. Not on our tight schedule. We had to pay our respects, then get on with the day's work. For me, that meant the first day of strawberry picking.

Daddy and the boys gathered sticks and broken branches and pulled weeds around our family headstones, while me and

Momma scrubbed them clean. When that was done, Momma placed flowers from her garden on each grave.

A few headstones date back to the 1800s, including a great aunt and uncle who were some of the first to settle in the valley. But the ones I cared most about were Grandpa and Grandma. Their headstones stood side by side, tucked in a far corner beneath a maple tree.

I never met Grandma. She had died during the flu pandemic of 1918, ten years before I was born. Even so, Grandpa told me so many stories about Grandma that I felt I knew her.

Grandpa missed Grandma so much. He always said he would be with her again someday. Now, he was. It nearly broke my heart when he died.

Grandpa had been my buddy, my constant companion growing up. The least I could do was take special care of his final resting place. I did the same for Grandma's. I knew Grandpa would want it that way.

We were at the cemetery for no more than fifteen minutes. Daddy said a little prayer before leaving. We all joined him at the end with an "Amen."

The truck rattled along back to the farm. I was glad to be sitting up front. It was only a few miles, but the boys in the back were cold clear through by the time we got home.

"Boys," Daddy said, eyeing Ed and Bill, "I want you two to get started on the south field after milking. I'll meet you there when I get back."

Momma and Marty were headed for the house. I was so excited and anxious about the new job that I wasn't sure what to do.

"Where's your lunch bucket, honey?" Daddy asked.

"In the house."

"Well, go get it."

"Yes, Daddy."

I ran to the house. I grabbed lunch out of the icebox, packed it in my pail, and hoofed it back to the truck.

"Okay, let's go," I said as I shut the truck door.

"Hold your horses," Daddy said.

"What are we waiting for?"

"Your brother."

"Marty? Why do we have to wait for him?"

"He's picking, too."

"But you never said …"

"That was part of the deal with Mr. Flanagan," Daddy interrupted. "I didn't consider saying anything to you about it. Didn't think it mattered." He looked me in the eyes. "Does it?"

I shook my head, even though it did matter. Somehow it seemed to take something away from me getting the job.

Marty opened the door and climbed in next to me. "Sorry I'm late, Daddy," he said. "Scoot over, Ruby."

I tried not to move over any more than I had to, partly to spite Marty but mostly to stay out of the way of Daddy's elbow when he shifted gears.

I hardly said a word all the way to the berry patch. On the other hand, Marty never shut up.

"I wonder how many flats I'll pick today. I bet I can pick ten. Yeah, ten. I'm going to pick ten." Marty wasn't talking to anyone in particular. He was just chattering, as he always did. "Of course, why should I settle for ten. If I can pick ten, it's not that many more to fifteen."

Oh, brother!

Out of the corner of my eye, I saw Daddy sneak a peek at Marty. He was trying not to smile.

"How much did Mr. Flanagan say he'd pay?" Marty asked.

"Twenty cents a flat," Daddy answered.

"If I pick ten flats, I would earn … er … ten times twenty …"

"Two dollars," I said. I couldn't help myself.

"Two dollars," he repeated, glancing at me, letting that number settle in his brain. I could see the gears turning in his head. "So, if I pick one hundred flats, that would be twenty dollars, right?"

Daddy let out a laugh. "Boy, if you can pick a hundred flats, you can pay Ruby and me to stay home and listen to the radio all day."

Marty gave Daddy a puzzled look.

"Look, son, it's great you're excited about picking and making money. Just don't get your hopes too high. A flat of berries takes a while to pick, especially for someone who's never done it before."

"Okay. Ten. I'll stay with ten."

"Five is a good number, too," Daddy said, obviously trying to get Marty to be more realistic. "It takes a lot of picking to fill five flats, but you can do it. That wouldn't be bad for your first day."

I didn't tell them my goal was ten flats, too. I hoped I could pick that many.

The truck jounced hard as Daddy turned off the valley road onto the dirt track leading to Mr. Flanagan's strawberry field.

Like most people in the valley, Mr. Flanagan had grown many different things over the years. But he was new to strawberries. He had mail-ordered the plants three years ago. As expected, there were few strawberries the first season, but the berries came on strong last year. Mr. Flanagan anticipated a bumper crop this year.

I hoped he was right. My money jar was counting on it.

Chapter 11

STRAWBERRY SHOWDOWN

Butterflies fluttered in my stomach as Mr. Flanagan walked Marty and me to our rows. He had already shown us where to get empty flats and where to take them when we finished filling them with strawberries.

"Hey, Marty! Over here!" It was Paul. "I saved you a row!" he hollered.

Marty looked at Mr. Flanagan.

"Go ahead," Mr. Flanagan said. "But no goofing off."

Mr. Flanagan led me past several more rows of strawberries with pickers already at work. Then we passed at least a dozen empty rows before he stopped.

"Here," he said, pointing. "I want you to start on this row. If you can't finish it, I'll have someone start at the other end and work toward you."

The message was clear: Mr. Flanagan thought I would pick slower than molasses in January. That's probably why he put me so far ahead of the other pickers. He figured they would catch up to me before I finished my row.

"Pick 'em like this," he said, kneeling on the ground and demonstrating how. "Got it?"

"Yes, sir."

"And no green ones. Not even a little green," he said. "No rotten ones either. They have to be berries you would eat."

Was that Mr. Flanagan's way of saying I could sample a strawberry now and then?

"And no eating the berries," he said, dashing my hopes. "Everything you pick goes in a hallock."

He stood up. "Understand?"

I don't know why he kept asking me things like I was stupid or something.

"Yes, sir," I said.

"My only other rule is no throwing berries," he said, putting his fists on his hips. "You throw berries, you get fired. No second chances. Got it?"

"Yes, sir."

There was a moment of uncomfortable silence as he eyed me.

"Well, go on. Start picking."

I sat in the row and picked how Mr. Flanagan had shown me. He watched a while, then started to walk away. But, before getting too far, he turned and said, "Hey, Red."

There was that awful nickname.

"Yes, Mr. Flanagan?"

"Don't make me regret my decision to let you pick."

"No, sir. I won't let you down." I said, smiling. I thought he might smile back, but he didn't.

I suddenly felt cold. Partly because of the cool reception, but mostly due to the cold morning and heavy dew soaking my overalls. My hands were wet and freezing already.

I tried to avoid the wet by picking the strawberries without touching the plants. That was impossible. Within minutes, my coat and shirt underneath were soaked to the elbows.

My backside was wet from sitting on the ground, so I

stood, straddled the row, and picked bending over. It was drier. Unfortunately, the blood rushed to my head, and my back got tired. I decided to kneel and pick, which worked better than the other positions, and that's how I picked for the first little while.

After it warmed up, I took off my coat, walked it to the end of my row, and covered my lunch bucket to shade it from the sun. I pondered my progress on the way back to my half-filled flat. I thought I'd been picking at a good pace but really hadn't gone far at all.

"Hello, neighbor!" called a voice. It was Mrs. Prescott. She was picking about ten yards behind me on the row next to mine.

"Hey, Mrs. Prescott."

"How are the berries?" she asked.

"There are lots of them. So many that I keep looking and looking to make sure I get them all."

"That's my girl."

It suddenly dawned on me: Maybe competition was what I needed to pick faster. I could race Mrs. Prescott!

I started picking as fast as my fingers would go and kept up the pace for at least a half-hour. Surely, I had pulled away from Mrs. Prescott by then. But when I looked behind me, there she was, only a few feet away.

"Hello again," she said.

"I give up," I said. I sat back on my heels and stared at the sky.

"What's the matter, dear?"

"I don't think I'll ever be good at this."

"Why do you say that?"

"No matter how fast I try to pick, I just don't get very far. Look at this," I said, motioning from where I sat to the start of my row. "It's mid-morning, and this is all the farther I've come."

Mrs. Prescott took off her hat and wiped her forehead with the back of her wrist. "You're a fine picker," she said. "I'm pretty good myself, but for the life of me, I couldn't catch up to you. You were working so hard."

"You don't have to try to make me feel better."

"Well, then, maybe I can offer some pointers."

"Like what?"

"There's always more than one way to solve a problem," she said as if she were teaching a lesson at school. "Maybe you just need to try something different."

"I've tried," I whined. "Do you really think there's hope for me?"

"I certainly do," she said, replacing her hat. "Why don't I start by showing you how I pick."

"That would be swell."

Mrs. Prescott knelt over a strawberry plant. She scooped her forearm under the vines on the far side of the plant and pulled them toward her. That one quick motion exposed the underbelly of the plant and dozens of red, ripe strawberries.

"Did you see how I did that?" she asked, picking the berries with both hands as she talked. "Instead of hunting and picking the berries one at a time, I went right to where the berries were hiding."

She repeated the process until she had flipped and picked around the entire plant. It didn't take her more than a minute or two to pick it clean.

I was amazed. Mrs. Prescott made it look so easy.

"What do you think? Do you want to give it a try?"

"Sure. I think I can do that."

"That's the spirit."

It took a while to get the hang of it, but soon my fingers were flying, and the berries piled up faster and faster. Mrs. Prescott was a few yards ahead of me by then, but I was gaining on her.

"I'm going to beat her to the end of the row," I told myself.

I was soon picking so fast it didn't take long to catch Mrs. Prescott and pass her. When I finished the row, I was way ahead of her, and I had picked four flats of strawberries.

"Looks like you're getting the hang of it," Mr. Flanagan said, walking me to a new row.

The rest of the morning flew by. I had picked three more flats by the time I sat down for lunch. That made seven flats altogether. As I ate, all I could think about was getting back to the field to pick more.

Lunch had recharged my batteries. Even though it was hot and there was no shade, I picked faster than ever.

I couldn't say the same for the other pickers. They were feeling the effects of the heat, picking in slow motion or no motion at all. But the heat was the least of my worries. I still needed three flats to reach my goal.

I was just finishing another flat when a strawberry streaked past me. It narrowly missed my head and splattered in the dirt not five feet away. It was a nasty, rotten one.

Marty. It had to be him. But when I turned to look, he had his head down, picking. I scanned the berry field looking for other suspects. The only problem was I had no idea what a berry thrower looked like.

Whoever it was, they didn't stop at just one. Strawberries continued to streak past me now and again. The good thing was, the person couldn't throw worth a hoot.

About two o'clock, I carried another flat of berries to the end of my row. It was my third of the afternoon and my tenth of the day. I had reached my goal and the day wasn't over yet.

I deserved a pat on the back. Instead, I got a fat, juicy strawberry. It hit me right between the shoulder blades.

I whipped around and caught Marty grinning at me. He didn't even try to hide his guilt. To my surprise, Paul was looking at me with the same stupid grin.

I shook my fist at them.

Marty made a face, then laughed.

"Serves 'em right if Mr. Flanagan catches them," I mumbled. I no sooner said it when a strawberry flew over my head. A second one hit me in the back again.

I don't know if it was because the berries were starting to hit me or because I knew who was throwing them, but I was getting mad. Real mad.

I tried to ignore Marty and Paul. Really, I did. But I had a temper and it was starting to get the best of me. After a few more hits and near-misses, it was all I could do to keep from losing my temper altogether.

In desperation, I turned and yelled, "Stop it!"

The words were barely out of my mouth when a strawberry slashed across my face and disintegrated in my hair. Juice and berry guts oozed down my cheek and dripped from my ear.

"That's it!" I screamed, jumping to my feet, both hands loaded with berries. I heaved one handful at Marty and the other at Paul. There was no way to tell if any berries hit their mark. I was too angry to care.

I scooped up another handful of berries and heaved it at them, then another and another. I lost count of how many I threw. It was enough to make my arms hurt from throwing so hard, but I didn't care.

"I'm! Sick! Of! It!" I yelled, throwing a handful to emphasize each word. "Stop! Throwing! Berries!"

In an instant, my rage was spent. I felt limp and out of breath but also relieved.

That's when I noticed a sudden calm. Marty and Paul were picking as if nothing had happened. I was suddenly baffled. Did the berry fight really happen? Or was it just a figment of my imagination caused by the heat?

When I looked around, I realized it was no figment of imagination. Everybody in the berry field—other than Marty and Paul—was staring at me.

"Uh, oh," I groaned.

What if Mr. Flanagan was looking at me, too? But then, why wouldn't he be? Not only had I thrown almost two hallocks of berries, but I had screamed like a banshee while doing it. I was afraid to turn around and look for Mr. Flanagan, but I did anyway.

Nope. Mr. Flanagan wasn't staring at me. But he was headed this way, almost at a run. When he turned down my row, there was no doubt about it. He had seen me.

Mr. Flanagan stopped and glared, the sun casting his shadow over me. "Come with me," he said, turning and stomping back the way he had come.

I dropped the strawberries in my hand, picked up my coat and lunch pail, and followed him without saying a word. It felt like a walk to the gallows.

When we got to his truck, Mr. Flanagan opened the wooden file box on the tailgate and pulled out a journal with a list of the day's pickers. There were tick marks next to the names to show how many flats each person had picked.

He ran his finger down the list until he came to my name. He counted the tick marks. His eyebrows raised. He adjusted his glasses and counted them again.

"I count ten flats, including the three stacked at the end of your row," he said. He reached inside the file box again and pulled out a small, metal money box.

"Ten flats," he repeated. "Is that right?"

I nodded, then added, "And six hallocks."

"Six hallocks?"

"The ones back on my row, where I stopped picking," I said nervously, trying to keep my voice from cracking.

He blinked at me. "Okay," he said, opening the metal box and grabbing the wad of dollar bills inside. He started to peel off two bills.

"Could I have it in coins, please?"

He gave me a funny look, then put the paper money back in the box. "Just like your grandpa, eh?"

"Yes, sir," I said.

Grandpa always said silver and gold were better than paper. He told me to take coins whenever I had a choice.

Mr. Flanagan fished around in his money box and then his pockets. "Here," he said, counting out a half-dollar, six quarters, and a dime. "Two dollars and ten cents. We good?"

"Yes, sir."

He took off his hat and wiped his brow. "Say. You wouldn't want to tell me who started the berry fight, would you?"

I shook my head. "No, sir. I'd rather not." I held my breath, hoping my answer wouldn't make him madder.

"I didn't think so," he said, rubbing his chin. "But don't you worry, I'll find out who it was sooner or later."

I felt relieved he didn't try to make me tell.

As I headed for home, my pocket full of coins jounced and jingled, playing a sweet tune with every step. It made me smile. I'd never earned so much money in one day.

Then I remembered why I was headed home in the first place. I'd been fired. The realization hit me like a mule kick to the backside. I had just ruined the best opportunity to earn the extra money I needed. Not to mention, how was I going to explain it when I got home.

Chapter 12

AN UNEXPECTED REACTION

As much as I wanted to, there was no way to avoid Momma and Daddy. When Marty came home from the berry patch alone, Momma got concerned and went looking for me. She found me down at the creek catching crawdads.

"Hey, how was your first day?"

"Fine."

"How many did you pick?"

"Ten and a half flats," I said, rolling onto my side, shielding my eyes so I could see Momma's reaction.

Her face lit up. "That's wonderful! I'm so proud of you, Ruby."

Too bad the conversation didn't stop there. If it had, I wouldn't have seen the disappointment on Momma's face when I told her I'd gotten fired.

The look on Daddy's face when Momma told him was even worse. I could tell it hurt him deeply. After all, he was the one who got me the job and vouched for me. I felt terrible for letting him down.

Daddy lectured me for twenty minutes. Momma grounded me for a week and gave me another list of extra chores.

It was just like before. Only worse. There was no school to break up the monotony, which meant I wouldn't see Virginia for a whole week.

Marty got grounded, too. I think it was on account of starting the berry fight. If that was true, I wondered how Daddy found out? I hadn't told him.

The mystery was solved the next day. I was coming down the stairs and overheard Momma and Daddy talking.

"Don't that beat all!" Daddy yelped, letting out a laugh.

It startled me, and I almost tumbled the rest of the way down the stairs.

"Keep your voice down, James," Momma said.

"Old man Flanagan said Ruby looked like a ten-armed windmill gone haywire," Daddy said, laughing again, but not as loud. "He said berries were flying everywhere. People were running and ducking. It must have been a sight."

My hand reached for the sudden tightness in my throat. I wasn't sure how I felt about what I'd heard. Not only because I was eavesdropping—not on purpose, mind you—but also because Daddy was talking about me. The funny thing was, he sounded almost proud.

"It's nothing to laugh about," Momma said in a low, serious voice.

"I know. It's just good to hear Ruby stood up for herself, that's all."

"Is that what you call it?"

"Oh, come now, Margaret. Ruby didn't start it."

"Maybe not, but we certainly don't want to encourage bad behavior."

"I know that." He let out a breath, like the sudden blast of air from a train engine.

It got quiet all of a sudden. I wasn't sure if I should stay or go.

"What else did Mr. Flanagan have to say?"

"Turns out Ruby is a star picker. A real natural."

"So I heard."

"Flanagan said she had the third-highest total."

"That's wonderful."

"Ain't it, though," Daddy said, sounding proud again. "Flanagan is heartbroken. He told me to make sure and bring her out next year."

"Maybe he'll hire her back this year."

"Not a chance. The rules are the rules with that old codger."

"That's too bad. Did Mr. Flanagan ever find out who started the whole thing?"

"Nope," Daddy said flatly. "He didn't see it start, and nobody would tell him anything."

"Then why were you so hard on Marty?"

"Because he started it."

"I thought you said …"

"I said Flanagan doesn't know. But Art Johnson knows."

"Art Johnson?" Momma asked. "You mean the man with the nice family who moved into the Baxter place?"

"That's right. Art stopped by to borrow a come-along. Evidently, his wife was furious about the strawberry stains on her son's shirt."

"I know that boy. Paul. He hangs out with Marty."

"Yeah, that's the one. Anyway, Art said he had to use a little persuasion to get the whole story. Paul eventually spilled the beans. He admitted throwing berries, but he said Marty started it."

"Well, tell that to Mr. Flanagan," Momma urged.

"I can't do that."

"Why on earth not?"

"Because it's up to the kids to work it out for themselves."

Momma and Daddy continued to talk, but I was done

listening. I didn't need another week tacked onto my punishment for eavesdropping. As quietly as I could, I snuck back up the stairs.

I never said a word to anybody about what I had overheard. Except for Virginia.

Chapter 13

CRAWDAD LESSONS

"Did your father really say that about letting Marty and Paul work it out for themselves?" Virginia asked.

"Sure did." I was only half-listening, my attention focused on a monster crawdad curious about my toes.

"What does your father expect them to do?"

"He's hoping they will do what's right and tell Mr. Flanagan how the berry fight started."

"Why would they do that? He'll fire them. Or worse."

"Daddy never said it would be easy."

Virginia hopped from the shore onto a small, misshapen boulder in the creek. "That's not what my parents would do if it were me."

The monster crawdad squirted under a rock.

I looked up. "They wouldn't?"

"Nope. My mother would go see Mr. Flanagan, tell him the whole story, and demand my job back."

I laughed. "That sounds like your momma."

For weeks, Virginia had been begging me to show her how to catch crawdads. Today was a perfect day, not just because of the weather, but also because she was staying the night and we had all day to do it. But she seemed more interested in talking than catching.

She crouched on the rock with her arms half spread for balance. She looked like a tall, featherless bird trying to get up the nerve to fly.

"There aren't any crawdads along here, are there?" she asked, peering into the water on the deep side of the boulder.

"Probably. Crawdads are everywhere."

While Virginia stood on her perch, I searched the bottom of the creek with the window box Daddy had built for me. It had a pane of glass mounted in the bottom so I could see underwater. The rest was made of cedar, which helped it float.

The creek was no more than waist-deep in most places along the shore. I could see the bottom clearly as I slowly searched, turning over rocks with my feet, looking for crawdads.

When I found one, I'd reach down and snatch it behind the head. I caught most of the ones I saw, but sometimes they got away. I hated when that happened.

"Arghhh!" I groaned, slapping the water.

Not only had I just missed catching two beauties, but Virginia seemed bored with crawdad lessons. I had taught her three or four ways to catch crawdads, but she hadn't caught a single one yet.

"I could really use your help. You haven't even gotten your feet wet."

"Is that right?"

Virginia stood up straight, stretched out her arms, and did a perfect shallow dive into the creek. Several seconds later, her head popped up in midstream. She flipped her hair to the side and smiled.

"Show-off!" I teased.

Virginia's smile melted. "I was not showing off."

"Looked like it to me."

"Don't you dare say that, Ruby!"

Show-off was an insult to Virginia. She'd been taught it wasn't proper to attract attention to yourself.

I started laughing. "Relax. I was only kidding."

Virginia swam toward me with her face in the water. She did a half-circle, then popped her head up. "There are two crawdads not four feet from your right foot."

"Thanks for the tip."

"You're welcome," she said. "Say, I've got an idea. Why don't I spot the crawdads and you grab them?"

"I got a better idea. Why don't both of us do both? We can catch twice as many that way."

Virginia wrinkled her nose.

"Okay. What's wrong?"

She looked away without answering.

"I know you can swim—like a fish—and I know you're not afraid of the water. So, what else is there?" Then it hit me. "Are you afraid of crawdads?"

Still no answer.

"Virginia?"

She looked up. "Well, now that you mention it."

I felt bad. I hadn't even considered the possibility.

"Don't be mad, Ruby."

"I'm not mad." I motioned her toward me. "Here, let me show you again how to catch them without getting pinched."

Virginia swam over and treaded water horizontally in the shallow water.

"It's much easier to do if you're standing up."

"I don't think so."

"Why not?"

"That's part of it, Ruby," Virginia said. She looked ready to cry. "I'm afraid to put my feet on the bottom."

"Oh. Okay. We'll have to work on that," I said, "but let's do it your way for now. You spot 'em, and I'll catch 'em."

Virginia smiled. "Okay."

I have to say, the system worked like a charm. Virginia had good eyes and didn't mind keeping them open in the cold water. We caught three times as many as if I'd been doing it by myself.

All told, we had more than forty crawdads in the bucket, including six monster-sized ones. Not bad for a couple hours of catching.

Chapter 14

ANOTHER FIRST FOR VIRGINIA

The minute Virginia walked through the kitchen door marked a momentous occasion. It was the first time she planned to stay the night.

Virginia and I had been best friends for more than a year, but she'd been to my house only twice, not counting the lemonade run.

I'd been to Virginia's house and stayed the night countless times. I suppose it was easier since she lived so close to school, and Mrs. Valentine seemed to prefer it that way.

Virginia lived in a nice place above the restaurant. It was almost new, filled with lots of pretties and all the latest conveniences, including indoor plumbing, and electric lights and appliances.

My house didn't have any of those things. Not yet anyway. It was older, too. Grandpa and Daddy built it forever ago when Daddy was courting Momma.

We didn't have a lot of money for things like new drapes or fancy wallpaper. But, of course, not many folks did these days.

Momma was busy stoking the cookstove when we came in from crawdad catching. I closed the screen door gently, so it didn't slap shut and startle her.

"Hi, Momma."

Virginia was right behind me. "Hello, Mrs. Ryan."

"Good afternoon, girls," Momma said. "How many did you catch?"

"A few dozen," I said.

"What do you have planned for the rest of the day?"

"I thought I'd show Virginia my room. Probably go back outside after that."

"Good day for it," Momma said, walking to the sink to wash her hands. "Just remember, I could use your help before supper, about four-thirty."

"Okay."

Virginia and I galloped up the stairs.

I pulled back the curtain in my doorway and gestured to my bedroom. "Here it is."

I felt an unexpected twinge of embarrassment as if seeing my room for the first time through someone else's eyes. It suddenly looked plain and bare.

Virginia stood transfixed, studying the exposed beams and rafters overhead. "Wow!" she said, finally, then flitted across the room like a honeybee checking out a field of new blooms.

"Oh, I love your bed," she said, caressing the pink and red roses on the iron bed frame. "It's beautiful."

"Thank you. It was Grandma's when she was a girl."

"And the view is gorgeous," she said, pausing at the window.

Virginia noticed and touched everything, from the photo of Patsy and me to my antique silver brush, and the hand embroidery on my pillowcases to my collection of painted rocks. She even poked through the row of books on top of my nightstand.

"Looks like we've read a lot of the same books," she said, swiping her finger across the titles printed on the spines. She pulled one out and sat on my bed, thumbing through the pages.

"*Doctor Doolittle.* That's one of my favorites," I said.

"Mine, too."

I sat down beside her.

"So, with no electricity, how do you have enough light to read? Father says kerosene and oil lamps aren't very bright."

"You get used to it. I prefer to read by daylight, but at night I have to use an oil lamp downstairs. Daddy doesn't allow lamps up here."

"Can we read tonight, after dark?"

"Sure. I suppose so."

"I just want to see what it's like. You know, reading as the pioneers did."

Ouch! I know Virginia didn't say it to be mean, but it hurt just the same. I had never thought of myself as one of the pioneers.

"You won't like it. Not after the novelty wears off," I said. "Electric lights are so much better."

Virginia gasped suddenly, startling me. She got up and bounded across the room.

"What's this?" she asked, running her hands over the rich, dark finish of the wooden box on my dresser.

"My writing box."

"It looks ancient."

"It is. Grandpa gave it to me when I was ten, just before he passed away. It was his daddy's and his granddaddy's before that."

Grandpa called it a writing slope. That's because the box formed a slanted writing surface when open, like a school desk. I thought of it more as a lap desk because you could balance it on your legs and use it as a desk almost anywhere

Grandpa had kept odds and ends inside, like important

papers and keepsakes. My favorites were his coin collection and the journals he and Daddy had written at my age. Everything but the papers was still inside, along with my own keepsakes. I planned to add my journal to the box at the end of the summer.

"It's beautiful," Virginia said, turning the key and opening it. She slid her hands across the velvet-covered panels that unfolded to make the writing surface. She opened the side drawer and fingered through the trinkets inside.

"There are so many nooks and cubbies."

"Let me know if you find a secret compartment."

She looked up with wide eyes. "Really?"

"That's what I think."

"So you don't know for sure?"

I shook my head. "No. It's just a feeling, on account of how Grandpa used to handle the box, and how he once told me to hold tight and protect its 'secret,' whatever that meant."

"Wow!"

"The box feels heavier than it should, too. At least, I think so. And sometimes, when I take everything out, something rattles inside when I shake it."

Virginia lifted the box and shook it with more than a little effort. "I see what you mean about the weight."

Virginia was so captivated by the box she wouldn't put it down. The only way to get her away from it was to promise she could use it to write something after supper.

I showed her the rest of the house, then the barn and farmyard. She wasn't much for the animals, especially the messes they left behind. It was funny to watch the pains she took to avoid them, even though she had boots on.

Virginia did like Rickabar. She had ridden him when she was here once before. We rode double. I remember she held on so tight I could hardly breathe.

"Want to try riding him by yourself today?"

Virginia wrinkled her nose.

"I'll walk alongside, ahold of the lead rope."

"I'd rather ride with you."

"Tell you what: Why don't we get you reacquainted with him, and then you can decide whether or not you want to ride by yourself or not."

Rickabar was a gentle old soul. I knew he'd win her over. After brushing and petting him a while, Virginia agreed to get on by herself and do a once-around the pasture. She liked it so much she wanted to do it again and again. After a while, she even braved doing it without me holding the lead rope.

"This isn't so hard."

"See. I told you."

"Why don't you get your other horse, and we can ride side-by-side."

"Hercules? Nah. He does all right hauling a wagon or pulling a plow, but he doesn't like to be rode."

"That's too bad."

"I've got an idea! How about we ride double on some trails?"

Virginia's eyes lit up. "Sure. Hop on," Virginia said, reining Rickabar to a stop. "I'll let you drive since I don't know where we're going."

As soon as I took the reins, Rickabar sensed what was coming next.

"Hold on."

Rickabar threw his head and did a little prance. When I gave him a squeeze with my knees, he took off at a gallop.

"Hey, this is fun!" Virginia shouted.

"Well, then, you're going to love this!"

I steered Rickabar sharp to the left, across a patch of sandy shore and into the creek. Water splashed everywhere.

Virginia squealed with delight.

I gave Rickabar free rein from there. He knew the way. He and I had ridden these trails hundreds of times. He headed for the upper pasture, working harder as he climbed the hill.

At the top, I reined him to a walk, and we rounded the foot of the bluff and disappeared into the cool, refreshing woods on the other side. We didn't return to the barn until we had explored nearly every trail, and I had shown Virginia all my special places.

Virginia couldn't stop talking about the ride. She chattered away as we walked Rickabar to cool him off, and she hardly stopped talking until after we had wiped him down and brushed him.

"That was fun," Virginia said, grinning. "Can we do it again tomorrow?"

"Maybe. What do you want to do now?"

We spent the rest of the afternoon doing things Virginia had never done before, like climbing trees and charming garter snakes, which took a bit of arm twisting. We even searched for birds' nests and animal tracks and wove baskets using whips of vine maple. The baskets weren't much to look at, but we were proud of them just the same.

We had so much fun we were almost late getting back to the house to help Momma. She was already in supper mode, bustling around the kitchen, trying to do three things at once.

Virginia and I peeled and sliced potatoes. Without a word, we started to race to see who could peel the fastest. It was something we always did when I helped at the restaurant.

When we had finished and the potatoes were boiling, we set the table. Momma had us use the Sunday china and silver on account of having company for supper.

My hope for a quiet family meal went out the window as soon as my brothers started arriving at the table.

"What are you doing in my chair?" Bill growled.

Marty looked up. Bill towered above him.

My little brother's not much for brains, but he's got guts. My guess is he stole Bill's seat so he could sit next to Virginia.

"I thought maybe we could trade places—just for tonight," Marty squeaked.

"Not on your life."

"I've got a nickel."

"Not interested," Bill said, grabbing the chair and pulling it and Marty away from the table. "Scram!"

"Please keep your voice down and mind your manners," Momma said as she hustled in with the last of the serving dishes.

"Sorry, Momma."

Bill glared at Marty, motioning with his head to leave.

Marty surrendered and sulked to his usual seat on the other side of the table.

Supper at the Ryan house usually wasn't a time for talking, but it was different when we had company. Everyone seemed to want to talk.

"So, Virginia, you enjoying your stay?"

"Yes, sir, Mr. Ryan."

"I showed her everything."

"You show her the outhouse yet?" Bill joked.

"William!" Momma growled.

"What?" he asked, playing innocent. I suppose it was my fault for telling him Virginia was squeamish about outhouses.

"We'll not have that kind of talk at the table."

"Sorry, Momma."

"Did Ruby tell you we are getting electricity this summer?" Daddy asked.

"Yes, sir."

"Pretty soon, the valley will be just like Crossroads," Ed chimed in.

"Yeah. Except the houses won't be as close together, and there'll be far more sheep and cows than people," Bill joked.

Momma gave him a stern look. "You'll have to excuse the messes," she said. "James is cutting holes in the walls and putting in the last of the wiring."

"I've cleaned up all the messes," I said defensively.

"You need to dust again, please."

I had forgotten about the plaster dust. It hung in the air for days and settled on everything. I'd be dusting for weeks before it was gone.

"Did you hear? The Germans captured Paris?" Bill said to no one in particular. He was always talking about the war in Europe. He said he'd be first in line at the enlistment office if the United States got involved.

Daddy stopped chewing. "Where'd you hear that, son?"

"Mr. Abbott. I heard him tell Mr. Thompson when I picked up the wire today."

"I knew it," Daddy said, stabbing a hunk of potato. "It was only a matter of time."

"No war talk at the table," Momma said.

The mood suddenly changed, and the room got quiet. Everybody knew the war was a sore subject with Momma.

After supper, we gathered around the radio in the front room. There was a long, awkward hush while we waited for the radio tubes to warm up and for Daddy to find a station.

There was a rule at our house: Only Daddy was allowed to touch the tuning dial after dinner. He liked having control. He also had the best touch for finding stations.

Daddy jumped around the dial searching for a station to lighten the mood. One minute we were listening to the news, the next minute it was sports scores or farm prices. Eventually, he settled on the Russ Morgan Orchestra show.

Virginia and I started dancing together. Marty cut in so he

could dance with Virginia. Ed soon asked me to dance, but it was just a way to ease into dancing with Virginia.

"May I cut in?" he asked, brushing past Marty.

I think Ed was sweet on Virginia, too.

It was great fun.

When Singin' Sam came on, Virginia, Marty, and I sang along, while Bill and Ed played checkers. Momma and Daddy sat together on the sofa, listening and tapping their toes to the songs.

The late-night news was all about the Nazis capturing Paris. The war had been raging for almost a year. Everybody said the United States would get involved sooner or later. I hoped they were wrong. I didn't want Bill to go off to war, or Ed, if the war lasted that long.

"Time for bed," Momma said. She didn't want to hear the war news and didn't think we should listen to it either. She had lost a brother in The Great War.

"Oh, Momma!" Marty whined. He liked mysteries, and he knew all the best ones were on late.

"Don't 'Oh, Momma' me. It's past your bedtime. That goes for you, too, Ruby."

"Yes, Momma."

I didn't mind having to go to bed. In fact, I was looking forward to it. Virginia and I could sit and talk in the dark and do all the things we did when I stayed the night at her house.

Maybe we could do something different, too, to make her stay memorable, like sneaking out on the front porch roof. We could sit in the moonlight and watch for shooting stars. What could be more amazing than that?

Chapter 15

NIGHT PAINS

I was crawdad catching with Henry. Only the crawdads were the size of lobsters, and Mr. Valentine was paying me a dollar apiece. I realized I was dreaming when Virginia's voice started coming out of Henry's mouth.

"Ruby? Are you awake? Ruby?"

"Wha-what?" I said, still caught between asleep and awake.

"It's stuffy. Can we turn on a fan?"

"Don't have one."

"Really?"

I yawned. "Nope. Remember, no electricity."

"Oh, yeah. I forgot."

Virginia was right: My room was hot and stuffy. The day's heat from downstairs had filled the attic. That was wonderful in winter, but not so good the rest of the year.

"Isn't there something we can do?"

"If Marty wasn't such a fraidy cat, I could ask him to open his window and get a cross-breeze going."

"What'd you say?" Marty asked from across the attic.

"Nobody's talking to you," I said.

"I heard my name."

"Never mind. Go back to sleep."

Marty didn't give me any smart-alecky back talk. He must have been tired or maybe sleep talking.

"Why don't you ask him?" whispered Virginia.

"It won't do any good. Marty's afraid to leave his window open."

"What's he afraid of?"

"Bats."

"Bats?!"

"Uh-huh. Ever since one got in his room. He found it hanging upside-down from one of the rafters."

"That's creepy."

"It wasn't so bad."

"How'd he get rid of it?"

"He didn't. I did. I borrowed Daddy's blacksmith gloves and grabbed the bat while it was sleeping." I yawned again. "It was neat."

"Ewww!"

"No. Seriously. Bat wings are swell-looking."

When there was no response from Virginia, I thought maybe she was ready to go back to sleep. I was wrong.

"Ruby?"

"Yes, Virginia?"

"Can you close the window?"

"I thought you were hot?"

"I am."

"Okay. If you're sure." I got up and pulled down the sash. I left it open just a crack, so we didn't suffocate altogether.

"Good night, Ruby."

"Night, Virginia."

Good thing I hadn't said anything about bats before we crawled out the window to stargaze. I'd have never gotten her out on the roof.

With the window closed, it would take forever for my room to cool down. By then, we'd be sweating like pigs. I don't know about Virginia, but I was already roasting with nothing but a sheet over me. It didn't seem to matter. I was nodding off again almost as soon as I closed the window.

"Ruby?"

My eyes popped open. Was I dreaming? Or did I really hear my name again?

A breeze whistled through the crack under the window. It was the only sound, other than Virginia's soft breathing.

"Ruby?"

"What, Virginia?"

"I gotta go."

I didn't look forward to a late-night run to the outhouse, but I could hear the distress in Virginia's voice. I exhaled loudly.

"Don't be mad."

"I'm not," I said. But I was frustrated. "I told you that you should have gone before bed."

"I didn't have to go then."

"Uh-huh," I groaned, rubbing my eyes. "You haven't gone since you got here."

"I know."

"What did you think? You could hold it forever?"

"No, I suppose not," she said. She was already standing by the bedroom doorway. "I'm really sorry, Ruby."

We tiptoed down the squeaky stairs as quietly as we could. When we got to the kitchen, I lit a lamp. On the way outside, Virginia stopped on the back porch.

"What are you doing?"

"Getting my shoes."

"You don't need shoes."

"Oh, yes, I do," Virginia said. She knelt and slipped on her shoes without tying them.

The grass was wet with dew, and the air was cool and damp. A thin umbrella of fog obscured the stars and quarter moon. I guessed it was about three o'clock.

We stopped outside the outhouse door. "Here," I whispered. "You take the lamp."

Virginia hated outhouses. She had a long list of reasons, even though she'd never been in one.

The lamp was turned down low, but it still cast a bright glow from inside the outhouse. The light showed through the cracks and knotholes and cast thin beams from the dozens of holes drilled above the door for ventilation. The way the light reflected off the mist hanging in the air, it looked like a halo encircling the outhouse.

I was admiring how pretty it looked when suddenly a scream came from inside.

"Ahhhhh!"

The next thing I knew, the door flew open and Virginia streaked past me. She didn't say a word, just raced toward the house. Her shoes flew off as she ran, her hair streaming behind her.

Laddie started barking.

"Virginia!" I hissed.

It was too late. She was already on the porch and gaining speed. She probably didn't stop until she was back in my room.

Laddie came trotting out of the darkness.

"Attaboy, Laddie. Good watchdog," I said, petting his head. "Now, go back to bed. Go on. Get!"

He sauntered back toward the barn.

I opened the outhouse door to retrieve the lamp. That's when a shadow moved inside and gave me a scare of my own.

"Bandit!" I growled, half startled, half angry.

Bandit used to be my pet raccoon until Momma made me let him go. I was ten, and he was just a baby then. He still came around occasionally. I didn't mind. It was good to see him—unless, of course, it was at three o'clock in the morning.

He sat beside the magazine rack, chittering away, holding the end of the toilet paper as if offering it to me. I let out a laugh, then quickly covered my mouth.

Momma would be furious if she saw Bandit playing with her toilet paper. She didn't like to use the mail-order catalog, so she made Daddy buy toilet paper. It was the one luxury she wouldn't live without.

"All right. You need to get out of here," I said as Bandit rambled toward me. I opened the door wide. "Shoo! Shoo!"

He waddled out the door.

"You're lucky it was me. Momma would have had your hide."

Bandit disappeared into the darkness.

I picked up Virginia's shoes on the way to the house and tiptoed up the back steps. When I got to my room, Virginia was in bed, pretending to be asleep. I didn't know what to say or if I should say anything at all. I figured I'd leave it to Virginia if she wanted to talk. Evidently, she didn't, and before long I nodded off to sleep.

Chapter 16

NOT A HAPPY ENDING

By the time Virginia and I got up, Daddy and the boys had already eaten breakfast and driven up the valley to set the last of the poles for the power line. Daddy was in charge today. Mr. Richardson was elsewhere with a crew of linemen, stringing wire and doing hookups to farms. They'd been doing that for weeks now.

Momma was busy making a second breakfast, just for Virginia and me.

"What was all the ruckus last night?" Momma asked as she flipped pancakes. "I thought I heard someone scream."

"Oh, that," I said. "That was nothing."

"Didn't sound like nothing to me. Woke the whole house."

I glanced across the table at Virginia. Her eyes were puffy and red. She was just about to say something when I beat her to it.

"Had to visit the outhouse," I said. "Got spooked is all. You know how a voice carries at night."

"Uh-huh," Momma said, walking to the table with a plate piled high with blueberry pancakes. She only made them on special occasions. She even opened the bottle of maple syrup her sister sent from Vermont, which said a lot about what

Momma thought of Virginia.

"It was me, Mrs. Ryan. I was using the outhouse when a raccoon appeared out of nowhere."

"Did he hurt you?"

"No. Just scared me. All I could think about were the things mother told me about raccoons and rabies."

"Rabies?" Momma said, alarmed. She sat down. "Honey, I don't think you have to worry too much about that. We've never had a case of rabies in the valley, and I've been here more than twenty years."

"It was Bandit," I said.

"Your Bandit?"

I nodded.

"I haven't seen him in ages," Momma said.

"He comes around once in a while."

"I don't know why that darn dog doesn't keep critters away."

"Laddie likes Bandit."

"Silly dog."

The three of us continued to talk about all manner of things. We must have sat there a half-hour or more.

Momma enjoyed the company, even if it was just a couple of twelve-year-olds. She was a people person. The only thing was, Momma rarely saw anybody but family during the week. Sunday-morning church was about the only time she got out of the house.

Momma gathered our empty plates and silverware and took them to the sink.

"What do you feel like doing today?" I asked Virginia.

"Can we go riding again?"

"Sure."

"What else you want to do?"

Momma cleared her throat. "I need your help for a couple hours, Ruby." Momma leaned over the table and started wiping it clean. "Since your Daddy and the boys are gone for the day, you and I need to bring in the sheep from the upper pasture."

"Can't we do it Monday?" I asked.

"Sorry. No can do. The sheep man's coming to shear them Monday morning."

"You want to help with the sheep?" I asked Virginia.

She wrinkled her nose.

"I didn't think so," I said, smirking. "Come on. Let's go ride before Momma finds something else for us to do."

Rickabar was a good sport. We must have taken turns riding him around the pasture a hundred times. He could have kept going all day. On the other hand, me and Virginia were getting sore and had to stop.

We grabbed the crawdad gear and walked bow-legged up the creek to a spot we hadn't been before. Thank goodness, it wasn't far.

"Watch this," Virginia said. She flipped bottom-up and disappeared underwater.

Virginia stayed under for a long time. When she finally came up, she was holding a crawdad. "Ta-da!" she trumpeted, grinning wide.

"Bravo!" I couldn't believe this was the same girl who was afraid of crawdads the day before.

Not to be outdone, I dove under and scanned the bottom. I didn't like to keep my eyes open in the creek. The cold water gave me a headache. But I couldn't let Virginia outdo me. When my lungs felt like they were about to burst, I popped out of the water, gasping for air.

"Did you get one?"

I held up my hands.

"Two!" Virginia shouted, giggling. "My word, Ruby Ryan, you are a crawdad-catching marvel."

She kneeled and bowed as if paying respects to a queen, her

head dunking in the water in the process. When she stood back up, her hair hung in front of her face, dripping water.

I couldn't help but laugh.

We spent the next hour talking and swimming and catching crawdads. We stayed until pruney toes and fingers signaled it was time to get out of the water.

Momma was working in the garden when Virginia and I got back to the house.

"Can we listen to the radio?" I asked Momma as we padded past her.

"Yes, but go easy."

"We will."

Saturday radio wasn't as good as Sunday. Mostly it was baseball, news, and farm stuff.

I'd never tuned the radio before. It wasn't as easy as it looked, but eventually, I managed to find something we liked.

"Don't you just love the radio?" I asked, tapping my foot to the music.

"Oh, yes. I could listen all day if mother allowed it."

"Wouldn't that be swell?"

"Uh-huh."

It wasn't long before Momma called us to lunch. It was a quick fruit-and-sandwich meal because she was in a hurry to take care of the sheep.

"Sure you don't want to come? You don't have to help. You can just watch."

"No thanks," Virginia said. "How long will you be?"

"I don't know. Two hours, maybe."

Virginia frowned.

"Don't worry. I'll finish as soon as I can," I said. "Go ahead and make yourself at home. You can grab a book from my room, or there are more on the bookshelf in the front room. Games and puzzles, too."

"I'm sure I'll find something to do."

Momma's voice echoed from the porch: "Ruby! Are you coming?"

"Gotta go."

Moving the sheep took longer than I thought it would. They were not cooperating. It was as if there were two lead sheep. Ten sheep would go one way, and the rest would go in the opposite direction.

When we finally got them to the lower pasture, I noticed Virginia watching us. She stood on the bottom rail of the fence, leaning over the top rail.

I waved.

Virginia waved back. Then she motioned for me to go to her.

Momma was having trouble with some of the sheep. I held up two fingers for Virginia. Two minutes. I hoped that was all it would take.

When Momma and I got everything untangled and the first group of sheep settled where they belonged, I said, "I'll be right back, Momma."

"Where are you going?"

"Virginia needs me."

Momma waved her approval.

I ran over to Virginia. "What's up?"

By now, Virginia looked anxious. "I don't know for sure. Maybe it's nothing, and you'll know the answer right off."

"Maybe. What is it?"

"Well," she said, hesitating, trying to figure out where to start. Then the words poured out in a rush. "It's the radio. I don't think I broke it. At least, I didn't do anything to break it. But I think it's broke."

"What?!" My voice echoed across the pasture.

Momma looked up.

"Don't be mad."

"Virginia. Just tell me what happened. Why did you say you broke the radio?"

"I didn't say that. Not exactly."

"What do you mean?"

"I had been listening to the radio for a couple hours when suddenly it went dead. I turned it off, then on again, but nothing happened."

My chin dropped. I wiped my sweaty face and left it cradled in my hands.

"Oh, no. So, I did break it?"

I looked at Virginia. "No. No. I should have told you about the radio."

"It's all right, then? I didn't break it?"

I shook my head. "No. You didn't break it. But you did run the battery down—which is almost as bad."

"Battery? I never thought of that."

"It's my fault. I should have warned you not to play the radio. Daddy figured the battery was getting low, so he's exchanging it for a fresh one when he goes to Thackeray on Monday."

"Are we in trouble?"

"You could say that."

"I'm sorry, Ruby. I feel terrible."

Not as bad as I felt. I didn't look forward to telling Momma about the dead battery, let alone Daddy.

That night, the mood at the supper table was the opposite of what it had been the day before. Instead of everybody chattering away, hardly a word was spoken.

It was on account of the dead battery. There'd be no radio tonight. None tomorrow, either. Not until Daddy exchanged the battery. He and Momma were disappointed in me, but the boys were downright angry and wouldn't talk to me.

"We'll talk about this later," Daddy had said when I told

him. I could tell he didn't say everything he wanted to, on account of Virginia standing next to me.

The silent treatment continued after supper. When Daddy drove Virginia home, he was quiet and distracted.

Virginia and I exchanged glances now and then, but mostly we kept our eyes straight ahead.

I held my breath all the way to Crossroads, hoping Daddy didn't start yelling at me until after we dropped off Virginia.

My heart ached for her. I knew Virginia felt awful because she thought it was her fault. But it wasn't. It was my fault. I should have warned her.

When we pulled up in front of the restaurant, Virginia had the door open and jumped out almost before the truck completely stopped.

"Thank you, Mr. Ryan. Bye, Ruby," she yelled, hardly looking back.

I scooched away from Daddy and closed the door. He whipped the truck around. The wheels spun out as we turned off the pavement onto the gravel and headed for home.

"Here it comes," I thought to myself. This would be the "talk about it later" time Daddy had mentioned earlier.

I waited. And waited. But nothing happened. No lecture. No yelling. Nothing. Just more of the silent treatment.

We were halfway home when I wondered if maybe Daddy was waiting for me to say something first.

"I'm sorry, Daddy." I was so scared the words barely squeaked out.

Daddy looked at me for the first time since we left the house. Then he did the most puzzling thing of all: He grinned.

"You know, the dead battery might actually be a blessing in disguise," he said.

Where did that come from?

"It got me thinking," he continued. "We spend a lot of time

listening to the radio. Maybe we should cut back a little. You know what I mean?"

I wouldn't call an hour or two of radio too much. I enjoyed listening to the radio. Actually, I'd like to listen more. But I wasn't going to say that to Daddy now, not with him not yelling at me.

"Whatever you say, Daddy."

That night, we sat around the front room in our usual places. But instead of listening to the radio, we had what Daddy called fun-and-games night. We talked and played hearts and rummy, and Daddy got out his guitar. We sang cowboy ballads he and Grandpa used to sing when they mined gold in the Sierra Nevada mountains.

It was great fun, but I still couldn't wait for Monday when the radio had a fresh battery. Better yet, I couldn't wait for electricity to get here, so we didn't have to worry about dead batteries at all.

Chapter 17

GOOD INTENTIONS GONE AWRY

As hard as times were for most families, it was even harder for others. No matter how much those folks worked and scrimped and saved, they never seemed to catch up, let alone get ahead.

That described the Loiola family. They had a farm in the upper valley. There were six kids. Cheryl was the oldest, a year younger than me. She reminded me of my sister, Patsy, because she was like a second momma to her four younger brothers and baby sister.

When I stopped by Mr. Abbott's store after a day of fishing with Henry, Cheryl was there ogling the candy in the showcase.

"Hi, Cheryl."

She jumped, startled.

"Oh, hello, Ruby."

"See anything you like?"

Her eyes lit up. "Oh, yes. Gumballs. You can chew one all day, put it on the bedpost at night, and pick up where you left off in the morning."

I smiled, nodding. "I like mint patties."

"Those are good, too," she said, bending down to see the

candy selection on the bottom row. "I could eat just about any of them."

"Me too."

"I've almost forgotten what they taste like."

I knew what she meant. Store-bought candy was a rare treat. Holidays, birthdays, and big paydays were about the only times I ever got any.

Cheryl was probably lucky to get any at all. Ever. That's what I meant about times being harder for some folks than others.

I fingered the coins in my pocket. Eighteen cents. I always knew how much I had with me, mainly because I didn't carry money very often.

There were three pennies, the dime Mr. Valentine paid me for washing Friday night dishes, and a lucky nickel I found in the road on my way into town today. It was one of those new Thomas Jefferson nickels.

While Cheryl was still looking at the candy, I pulled out the nickel and pretended to pick it up off the floor.

"Look what I found," I said, holding up the nickel.

"Oh, my," she said, gasping. "What luck!"

"I think you dropped it."

She seemed surprised. "No. No, I didn't," she said.

"Well, I know I didn't lose it."

"I've never even seen a nickel like that."

"Here," I said, handing it to Cheryl. "Have a look."

She rubbed the nickel between her thumb and forefinger to feel the contours and shiny, smooth finish. She squinted at the detail. "It's so pretty," she exclaimed.

"It's not bad," I said. "Buffalo nickels are prettier."

"Those are beautiful, too," she agreed.

A nickel was a lot of money, and I'm not one to part with it easily, especially since I hadn't earned enough for my secret surprise yet. But this was different. The nickel wasn't mine to begin with. I found it. The way I figured, Cheryl could just as easily have found it.

Mr. Abbott appeared behind the counter. "Hello, Ruby, Cheryl. What can I do for you two?"

"Cheryl wants to buy some candy."

"No, not me," she said, looking embarrassed and confused. "I mean, I do, but I don't have any money."

"What's that in your hand?" Mr. Abbott asked. "Looks like a nickel to me."

"It's not mine."

"What she means," I said, interrupting, "is we found it."

Cheryl looked at me.

I nodded at her. "You and me."

"Is it okay if we keep it?" she asked Mr. Abbott meekly.

"Nobody said anything to me about losing a nickel in here," Mr. Abbott said.

"Then it's okay?" Cheryl asked.

"Fine by me—just as long as you spend it here," Mr. Abbott joked, chuckling. His face snapped back to attention when Cheryl's momma strutted up to the counter.

"Prices just keep going up, don't they?" Mrs. Loiola said, shaking her head. "And as for fabric, I wish you had more selection, Mr. Abbott, and something less expensive. Times are hard, you know."

"Yes, ma'am. I know. Fabric prices are high for me, too."

"Hi, Mrs. Loiola."

"Oh, hello, Ruby. I saw you and Cheryl drooling over the candy."

"Is it okay if I buy some, Momma?" Cheryl asked.

"If money grew on trees, I'd buy you all the candy you could eat, Sugar."

"Looks like Cheryl has money of her own," Mr. Abbott said.

Cheryl held out the nickel for her momma to see.

"Where did you get that?"

Before Cheryl could answer, Mrs. Loiola snatched the nickel from her hand and examined it.

"Found it," Cheryl said.

Mrs. Loiola studied Cheryl, then looked at the nickel again. Finally, she popped open her coin purse, dropped the nickel in, and snapped the purse shut.

"But, Momma ..."

"Don't 'but' me, Cheryl," Mrs. Loiola said. "I'm grateful you found it—I truly am—but I shouldn't have to tell you we don't have money to fritter away on candy. I'm sorry, Sugar, that's just the way it is. Now, come along. You can help me pick out fabric for your brother's shirt."

Mrs. Loiola turned and strode away.

Cheryl didn't know what else to do but follow. "Sorry, Ruby," she said as she left.

Mr. Abbott cleared his throat. "That was nice what you tried to do, Ruby."

"What's that?"

"Don't be coy with me, young lady. I saw you pull that nickel out of your pocket and pretend to find it."

"Oh, that," I said. I felt my face turn red. "I wanted to brighten Cheryl's day, that's all. She hardly ever gets anything extra."

"Just the same, it was a nice gesture," Mr. Abbott said. "I get your meaning. Like Cheryl's mother said, times are hard. I see it every day."

"Uh-huh."

"Now," Mr. Abbott said, "you came in here intent on something other than good deeds. What was it?"

"Oh, nothing. I just came to look around."

He smiled. "I see. Well, anything else I can do for you? Candy?" he asked, tapping on the counter above the mint patties.

I shook my head. "No, thanks."

"All righty, then," he said, checking to make sure the pencil was still behind his ear. He stooped and grabbed an order pad from under the counter. "I'm going to see if I can help Mrs. Loiola find some fabric."

"Okay."

"Say hello to your dad for me," Mr. Abbott said as he headed for the back of the store.

"Will do, Mr. Abbott."

As I turned to leave, I saw my secret surprise. It was hiding in plain sight in the front window of the store. Knick-knacks and glassware on display around it cast green, blue, and pink light across its surface.

One look and I knew all over again I had to have it. I ran my hand across it as I passed.

A sign on top said, "Like new. $29.49. Sorry, no trades or layaway."

Few adults had that kind of cash money, let alone a kid. That may be why I hadn't told Mr. Abbott my secret. He probably wouldn't think I could earn that much. Most folks wouldn't.

Maybe so. Maybe not. It didn't really matter what anybody thought. The fact was I didn't have the money yet, and I was running out of time.

Chapter 18

TWO SURPRISE ENCOUNTERS

The bulletin board outside Mr. Abbott's store was a popular attraction. All kinds of notices found their way there. Mostly things for sale or trade, or requests for sewing patterns or recipes. Occasionally, a job was posted. That always created a stir. It was a hopeful sign that things were getting better.

Virginia and I used the bulletin board, too. We left coded messages for each other. Like today. Virginia left a note saying she was shopping in Thackeray with her momma.

Unfortunately, that put a kink in my plans. Guess I should have checked to make sure she would be around before making the trip to Crossroads. I was about to head home when Mr. Valentine came running out of his restaurant.

"Ruby! Ruby!" he shouted. "Do you have a minute?"

"Hi, Mr. Valentine." I stopped and waited for him.

By the time he caught up to me, he was out of breath.

"What can I do for you?" I asked.

"I need crawfish," he wheezed.

"Oh, sure. Piece of cake."

"No. No. You don't understand," he said, his face so serious the lines on his forehead were as deep as a fresh-plowed field.

"I need *lots* of crawfish. But they must be le mieux—the best. You understand, the big ones. As many as you can catch."

That got my attention. I knew the crawdads Mr. Valentine was talking about. They were twice the size of average crawdads.

"I can pay you two—no, no—three times the usual rate. What do you say?"

Mr. Valentine waited with his hands on his hips as I tried to calculate how much money that would be. I figured I could catch maybe two or three dozen of the big ones if I had enough time and a little luck.

"Well?" he prodded, studying my face.

I was so excited about his offer that it was hard to concentrate. My brain couldn't seem to calculate.

Mr. Valentine mistook my slow response as a ploy to get more money.

"Okay. Okay. Five cents apiece. That's my final offer," he said, folding his arms across his chest. "Yes. Five cents. But they must be prime crawfish. Prime. What do you say?"

What else could I say? "You've got a deal, Mr. Valentine."

He smiled and shook my hand so hard I thought my arm was going to come out of its socket.

"Thank you, Ruby. I knew I could count on you."

"So, how many do you want?"

"I need six dozen."

The number hit me like a baseball bat. "How many?"

"Six dozen," he repeated, nodding. "That should do it."

Only one or two out of every ten crawdads I caught were big ones. I would have to search far and wide to find six dozen.

"And I need them Friday morning," he added. "You can bring them when you come to visit Virginia."

My head started shaking. At first, I didn't even realize I was doing it.

"What?" he asked. "Is there something wrong?"

Mr. Valentine was my best customer. I didn't want to tell him I couldn't do it, but I had to let him know what I was up against.

"Those aren't your average crawdads," I said, grasping for the right words.

"Yes, I know. That's why I want them."

"I mean, I don't come across a lot of them, and it will take time. Lots of time."

Mr. Valentine cocked his head and studied my face. "What are you trying to say? Do you want more money?"

"No! No, it's not that."

"What, then?"

My brain twisted itself into a knot trying unsuccessfully to figure out the right words to say. So, I just came out and said it: "I don't know if I can catch that many in only three days."

Mr. Valentine frowned.

"I mean, I will work very hard and find as many as possible, but I can't promise six dozen."

He rubbed his chin. "I tell you what," he said, "Bring me what you can. I'll pay you a nickel each for the big ones and nothing for the regular-size ones."

He studied my face as he waited for a response.

His stare made me squirm. I was sure I could catch maybe half that many big ones, so a nickel a piece for them—and nothing for the small ones—was still better than the usual price of a penny apiece. But I wanted to fill the whole order. It would mean a lot more money, and it would make Mr. Valentine very happy.

But he wasn't done wheeling and dealing. "And, if you fill my order completely—for six dozen jumbo crawfish—I will pay you the agreed price, plus a bonus of six bits more. How 'bout it?"

How could I say no? "Okay. I'll do it," I said.

"Fine. Fine," Mr. Valentine said, gloating.

"So, what's the occasion?"

"I have a special guest coming to the restaurant. Very special."

"Who is it?"

"I can't say."

I thought he was joking. "Really?"

Mr. Valentine shook his head.

"I thought we were partners," I teased.

"I tell you what. I will reveal the visitor's identity after they leave. How's that?"

"Oh. Okay."

"I'm sorry. That's the best I can do. I've probably said too much already."

"I understand."

"And you can't say a word to anyone." He put his fingers to his lips and twisted them as if turning a key in a lock. "Promise?"

"I promise."

"Good," he said, smiling. He patted me on the head. "Now, I must get back to my kitchen. I have lamb chops in the oven."

All the way home, I thought about Mr. Valentine's crawdad order. I was so distracted I hardly noticed the gathering storm clouds.

But instead of distant thunder, it was Buster's bark that interrupted my thoughts. I had just passed Mr. Wilson's corner fence post.

"It's okay, Buster. It's just me!" I shouted the way I always did when I passed.

When I got to Mr. Wilson's drive, I was surprised to see Buster standing on the porch rather than lying down. Usually, he didn't bother to get up when he barked at passersby. What surprised me even more was when he started to walk toward the road. Then he began to trot.

A chill went through me. I started walking faster.

"Hello, Buster! Hey, boy!" I shouted nervously as I lost sight of him.

I kept looking behind me.

A jolt of fear surged through my body when Buster appeared on the road. He had never done that before. And he didn't stop there. He kept on coming, barking and growling and baring his teeth.

My heart started to pound. I tripped and almost fell backward, which set off an instant panic.

Buster was a big dog and had always had a mean bark, but he never gave me a reason to fear him before. But, now—I was terrified.

Buster wasn't more than twenty feet away from me when a shrill whistle came out of nowhere. He stopped in his tracks, turned, and looked back toward the house. He gave me one last bark, then trotted away.

When I got home, I told Momma and Daddy about my encounter.

"Could it be your imagination is getting the best of you?" Daddy asked.

"No, Daddy. It's true. Buster was coming after me."

"I've been around that dog hundreds of times and never known him to be aggressive."

"Me, neither. But he was acting different today."

Daddy shook his head and rubbed his neck. "Well, if that ever happens again, you have to show Buster who's boss."

"How do I do that?"

"Well, whatever you do, don't run. He'll want to chase you."

I nodded. I'd heard that before, not just about dogs but about other animals, too.

"You can't let him know you're afraid, either," Daddy said.

"Stand your ground. Speak loud and firm. Use words he knows, like his name, and 'stop' and 'no.'"

"I don't know," I said, unsure that any of those things would have stopped Buster.

Daddy frowned.

"I'm sorry for being such a scaredy-cat."

Daddy mussed my hair. "Don't fret," he said. "Maybe Buster was having a bad day. It may never happen again."

"But what if it does?"

"Look, honey," he said, squatting down to my level. "You shouldn't have to be afraid. I'll talk to Mr. Wilson. In the meantime, you can ride with me whenever I go to Crossroads if you like."

"Nah. Thanks just the same, Daddy. I'll walk," I said. "You're probably right. Buster must have been having a bad day."

I was glad I talked to Daddy. He made me feel better—a little. The next time I walked to Crossroads, I would see if his advice worked or if I would even need it.

Chapter 19

ESCAPE FROM THE UNIMAGINABLE

I went right to work on Mr. Valentine's order, devoting every waking hour to the quest. No body of water was overlooked. No river rock was left unturned.

I spent twenty-eight hours searching. It was exhausting work, but by the end of the week I had caught enough monster crawdads to fill the order—all six dozen of them.

The crawdads were carefully packed and layered in wet burlap in a large bucket. Daddy lashed the bucket to the pack frame he used for hauling meat on hunting trips. I was using it to haul my load to Crossroads. All told, it weighed about twenty pounds.

Daddy was too busy to drive me, but we figured I'd be able to catch a ride before I walked far. Besides, I hardly felt the weight on my back as I crunched along the valley road. Why would I? I was floating on air. I'd just done the impossible and felt fantastic.

That feeling evaporated in an instant when I came within sight of the fence post that marked the corner of Mr. Wilson's property. It was replaced by a sense of dread.

This was the first time I'd walked past his place in three

days. In all that time, I hadn't once thought of being chased by Buster. Now, it was the only thing I could think about.

I told myself all I had to do was walk from one corner post to the other and everything would be all right. But as I got closer, I was having doubts that settled in the pit of my stomach like a pile of bricks.

Right on cue, Buster started barking as I passed the corner post.

"There's nothing to be afraid of," I told myself, saying it out loud as if that would make it so.

My face felt hot. Sweat popped out all over my body. A sour taste filled my mouth, and I suddenly felt sick.

"Hi, Buster! Hey, boy!" I called as I came within sight of Mr. Wilson's drive. I figured it was best to stay with the routine that had always worked before. Just the same, I crossed to the other side of the road.

I was walking fast, but my heart was racing even faster. I kept my eyes fixed on the spot where the driveway met the road.

The top of Mr. Wilson's house came into view. Then, the porch. As I crossed in front of the drive and could see all the way to the house, I spotted Buster standing on the porch in alert mode. He lifted his head when he saw me.

Before I could be thankful Buster was still at the house, he jumped off the porch and started to trot this way.

My heart stopped.

"Don't run," I reminded myself. "Don't run."

Even so, I couldn't help but walk faster.

Once Buster was out of sight, a glimmer of wishful thinking flashed in my mind. Maybe Buster would stop. Perhaps if I hurried and put enough distance between him and me, he would lose interest by the time he got to the road.

My hopes were dashed when Buster appeared. His eyes locked on mine, and he went from a trot to a full-out sprint.

His back legs almost came out from underneath him as he rounded the corner onto the road, his paws sending dust and gravel flying.

Terror seized my heart. While I felt the urge to turn and run, I didn't have any trouble standing my ground. That's because I couldn't move. I was frozen with fear.

It was an eerie feeling. I was as focused on Buster as he was on me, like we both had tunnel vision. I didn't hear or see or sense anything other than him charging toward me.

Every muscle in my body tensed and I screamed at the top of my lungs, "No, Buster! Stop!"

My words had no effect. Buster kept right on coming, barking like a crazed dog, his lips curled back to show his teeth, with drool hanging from each jowl.

He closed the distance between us in the blink of an eye. That's when everything started to move in slow motion.

Buster jumped and sailed toward me like a balloon on a stiff breeze. I instinctively put out my arms, stepped backward, and spun to the side like a matador avoiding a charging bull.

Buster brushed past me, his teeth snapping shut on nothing but air. He was so close I could feel and smell his dog breath.

I spun another quarter-turn like a slow-motion ballerina to prepare for the next attack I thought might come. Sure enough, Buster had already turned and was charging again.

Words and screams blurted out of my mouth without thought, fueled by fear and adrenaline, as Buster lunged for my legs this time. Reacting without thinking, I blocked him with a knee in the chest and pushed off with my near arm, narrowly missing being bitten.

My heart was in my throat by now, a sheen of nervous sweat on my hands, arms, and legs, and I could feel sweat streaking my face and trickling down my spine. I knew I'd been lucky. Twice. Odds were, I might not be so lucky a third time.

As Buster was about to attack again, Daddy's words echoed in my head: "Don't run." That advice couldn't possibly apply to this situation. Could it?

Another voice screamed inside my head: "Run! Run!"

So, I ran!

And Buster chased.

I ran for all I was worth, hoping that if I made it to the far post of Mr. Wilson's property that Buster would stop. How silly! I knew that wasn't going to happen, even if I could make it. Which I couldn't.

The load on my back slowed me down, the crawdads scraping and rattling against the metal bucket as I ran. Buster was closing fast. It was only a matter of seconds and he would catch me.

Then, it happened. Again. A loud, shrill whistle.

I was never so glad to hear it.

Buster stopped in an instant, just like before. But this time, he kept on snarling and barking. Maybe it was because I was still running. I don't know. Whatever the reason, I was too scared to slow down.

He was nowhere in sight when I finally stopped and looked behind me. My heart was pounding. Snot was running from my nose and I had a nasty, iron taste in my mouth. My legs felt like rubber.

I didn't stop for long, no more than a minute to catch my breath and gather my wits. Then I was off again. I wanted to put as many miles as I could between Buster and me.

I was still in shock when I got to Virginia's house. In fact, I don't even remember Mr. Valentine's reaction when I gave him the jumbo crawdads, or what was said when he paid me. The money in my pocket was the only proof it had happened at all.

Virginia and I had planned to catch crawdads, but that would have given me too much time to think about Buster.

We played games and talked instead.

I wanted to forget what had happened, but Virginia kept bringing the conversation back to Buster. She wanted to know everything. So instead of avoiding the subject, we talked and talked about vicious dogs. Mad dogs. Rabid dogs.

I was never so glad to leave Virginia's house.

I caught a ride with Mr. Abbott instead of walking. I'd had enough of Buster for one day.

Daddy got an earful when I got home. At first, he didn't seem to believe me. Who would? Buster had never done anything like that before. Not that any of us knew.

Then, Marty chimed in, "I heard Buster chased some boys the other day. Bit one of them."

Daddy got a concerned look on his face.

"You sure about that?"

Marty nodded. "Pretty sure."

Daddy rubbed his face. "I'll stop by and have a talk with Mr. Wilson. In the meantime, no walking to Crossroads. Neither of you. You get a ride with me or one of the neighbors. Understood?"

"Yes, sir," we said in unison.

He didn't have to tell me twice. In fact, I didn't know if I wanted to walk past Buster's house ever again.

Chapter 20

MYSTERIOUS VISITORS

Usually, after washing Friday night pots and pans at the restaurant, Virginia and I spent the rest of Saturday morning goofing off. Or we'd go down to Mr. Abbott's store and help him sort mail or flip through his mail-order catalogs and dream about things we couldn't afford to buy.

We weren't doing any of those things today. Other than for breakfast, we hadn't left Virginia's room. We just sat around reading and playing cards, the whole time me wondering why Virginia was acting so peculiar.

I'd been watching her since mid-morning. She had been quiet and preoccupied, but mostly it was the way she kept looking out her bedroom window that tickled my curiosity.

"What's so interesting?" I asked.

Virginia quickly turned away from the window. "What? Ah, nothing," she said. Her eyes darted around the room, looking everywhere but at me.

I smirked and put my book down. "You could have fooled me. That's the third time in ten minutes you've gotten up to look out the window."

Virginia shrugged, then walked back to her bed and jounced

down beside me. She leaned back against the wall, opened her book, and pretended to read again.

Don't get me wrong, I loved to read, but not on such a beautiful day. Besides, there was something Virginia wasn't telling me.

I got up and walked to the window to have a look for myself. I watched Virginia to see how she would react.

She pretended not to notice.

The window had a view of the church and school and the fields behind the houses and businesses that lined this side of the highway. Virginia's house—and her father's restaurant downstairs—was smack dab in the middle of Crossroads, three doors down from where the valley road intersected the highway.

While I stood there, an automobile rounded the corner of the building and crunched across the gravel parking area behind the restaurant. It was one of those half-car, half-truck automobiles with wood panels on the sides.

The driver opened his door, got out, walked to the other side, and opened the back door. Two men got out. I didn't recognize them. All three men wore hats, so it was hard to see their faces.

"Hey, Virginia. Are these the guys you were watching for?"

Quick as a sneeze, she was off her bed and standing beside me at the window. We watched as the men talked a while. We could hear them, but couldn't make out what they were saying.

"Well?" I asked.

"Well, what?"

"Are they the ones?"

"I don't know what you mean."

"You know what I'm talking about. You've been watching for someone or something all morning."

Virginia clammed up.

"Come on, Virginia. Tell me what's going on."

"Okay. Okay," she said. It was the first time she had looked at me since I started asking questions. "Promise you won't tell anybody?"

"I knew it!"

"Shhhhh! Ruby, please!" she said, grabbing my shoulders and putting her face close to mine. "Promise me. Not a soul."

I thought she was being melodramatic, but I played along. "Okay, I promise."

Virginia looked out the window. My eyes followed hers as I waited for her to start talking. We watched the two passengers walk to the restaurant's rear door, while the driver went back and sat down behind the wheel.

"Virginia, tell me what's going on," I pleaded. "Who are those guys? And why's it such a big secret?"

She whirled around, her eyes big and wild-looking. "It's the president," she exclaimed.

I was dumbstruck. I didn't know whether to laugh or to call her a liar.

"The president?"

Virginia nodded earnestly.

"The president of the United States?"

"Uh-huh," she said.

I started to chuckle. It had to be a joke. Right? Why would the president be here? But I never quite got to the point of outright laughing because Virginia didn't crack a smile, didn't even flinch.

"You're not kidding, are you?"

Virginia shook her head.

"One of those men is President Roosevelt?"

"No, the last one."

"President Hoover?"

She nodded and continued nodding as a smile spread across

her face. "Isn't it wonderful?" she said, giggling. Then, in one quick motion, she put her hands together and raised them to her lips as if praying. "But you can't tell a soul."

"I won't."

"Promise?"

"I already promised, didn't I?"

Virginia was transformed. She had been quiet and distracted all morning. Now, she was bubbling with energy.

"Let's go downstairs and see," I said.

She was suddenly serious again. "Oh, no. No."

"Why not?"

"Father told Emeline and me to stay in our rooms. He forbade us to go downstairs."

"Oh, come on."

"No."

I grabbed her by the shoulders. "Where's your sense of adventure?"

"Not downstairs."

"Oh, please? When will you ever have another chance to see a president in person?"

Virginia didn't say anything. She looked around the room, as if looking for an answer.

"Well?" I nudged.

"Let me think about it."

"Oh. Okay." I'm sure she could hear the disappointment in my voice. I flopped back down on the bed. I figured I could read some more while Virginia tried to make up her mind.

Virginia glanced out the window, then grabbed her book and sat down beside me. She never opened it, though. She was too deep in thought for the next ten minutes.

"Well?" I asked, too impatient to wait any longer.

"I don't know, Ruby," she sighed. "I've been thinking and thinking, but I still don't know what to do. I want to see the president. I do. But I don't want to upset father."

"We could sneak down. Your daddy wouldn't even know we were there."

"I don't know, Ruby."

"Come on. You know you want to." I said. At the same time, I couldn't help but feel for Virginia. I'd never seen her so distressed. Maybe I was wrong to push her. I was almost convinced of that until Virginia made up her mind.

"Oh, all right, let's do it," she said. Then in a firm voice added, "But we're only going to look. And you have to follow me and do as I say. All right?"

"Sure. Okay." I was so excited. I crossed my heart, spit in my hand, and held it out to Virginia. She stared at it, hesitated a moment, then spit in her hand as politely as you please, and we shook on it.

Funny thing, no sooner was the deal done and we both started having second thoughts. I kept wondering what would happen if we got caught. I think Virginia had the same concern.

We stood by the door to the downstairs for the longest time. Ten minutes passed before we finally mustered the courage to open it.

Chapter 21

CALL ME MR. HOOVER

Virginia and I tried to be quiet, but nothing cooperated. The upstairs door creaked something awful when we closed it behind us, and on the way down, every step squeaked like an out-of-tune violin.

I thought for sure somebody would hear us.

We stopped at the bottom of the stairs to listen, to make sure the coast was clear.

"My gracious, man, this has to be the best crawfish I've ever eaten," someone bellowed. "Sweet, yet spicy."

"Why, thank you, Mr. President," Mr. Valentine said.

"I haven't been president for quite some time. Please. Call me Mr. Hoover."

"Or the Chief," injected another man's gravelly voice, chuckling. His mouth sounded half full of food.

"Very well, Mr. Hoover," Mr. Valentine said.

"Good. Now let's have another helping of those delicious mudbugs."

Mr. Valentine had called him Mr. President, but I couldn't tell if it was really President Hoover or not. The voice didn't sound like the crackly, tinny voice on the radio and in newsreels.

I leaned around Virginia and tried to get a look. She elbowed me back. She turned, holding a finger to her lips, then pointed at the cart stacked high with pots and pans we had washed that morning. She motioned me to follow.

Virginia scurried toward the cart on tiptoes to keep the heels of her shoes from tapping on the floor. I followed so closely that I bumped into her when she stopped suddenly behind the cart.

She turned and gave me a dirty look.

I shrugged. I couldn't help that I was bubbling over with excitement and anticipation.

Virginia peered around one side of the cart, and I snuck a peek around the other side. Sakes alive! It really was him! Mr. Hoover, the former president of the United States. He was sitting no more than twenty feet away.

When I turned to see Virginia's reaction, I accidentally bumped the cart with my shoulder. Oh, no! The pots and pans on top leaned and wobbled, then toppled over.

Crash!!!

I cringed, covering my ears and squeezing my eyes shut as the rest of the pots and pans hit the floor in singles and pairs.

Clang-clang! Bong! Clatter-clatter-clatter!

When the racket finally stopped, I opened my eyes. There sat Mr. Hoover and the other man blinking in disbelief. Mr. Valentine stood beside the president, glaring.

I straightened up. "Hello," I squeaked, not knowing what else to say.

Mr. Hoover dropped the crawdad he'd been eating. "That's quite an entrance," he said, wiping his fingers and mouth with the napkin tucked in his collar.

"Ruby!" Mr. Valentine huffed. "And Virginia! I told you to stay in your room. You know better than to disobey me."

Mr. Hoover started chuckling, though I don't know why. I didn't see anything the least bit funny.

"Now, now, Pierre," Mr. Hoover said, pulling the napkin out of his collar and tossing it on the table. "It's quite all right."

Mr. Valentine nodded politely to Mr. Hoover, but he looked fit to be tied.

"Would you be so kind as to introduce me to these charming young ladies?" Mr. Hoover asked. "I'm sure they can keep our little secret. Can't you, girls?"

Virginia and I nodded eagerly.

Mr. Valentine motioned for us to stand beside him.

Virginia went and stood on one side of her father and I stood on the other. It was right about then that I noticed my face getting hot. But I couldn't have looked any more embarrassed than Virginia. I'd never seen her turn so red.

"Mr. President—I mean, Mr. Hoover—may I introduce my daughter, Virginia," he said, putting his arm around her shoulder.

Virginia forced a smile. It looked more like a cringe, probably because of the embarrassment.

"How beautiful," Mr. Hoover said. "I see the resemblance, Pierre. She has your eyes."

Mr. Hoover certainly didn't talk like a president, not how I'd heard him speak on the radio. He sounded more like a stuffy version of Grandpa.

"And this," Mr. Valentine said, patting me on the head, "is Virginia's clumsy friend, Ruby Ryan."

I felt a fresh gush of embarrassment.

Mr. Hoover chuckled. "I'm pleased to meet you both."

"I'm charmed, as well," said the man sitting beside Mr. Hoover, smirking.

Mr. Hoover cleared his throat and gestured to the man. "This is a friend of mine. A longtime fishing companion," he said. "We're headed to the coast and to do some fishing along the way."

There was a moment of awkward silence. After all, what are you supposed to say to a former president? For that matter, what does he say to a couple of nosy kids?

It wasn't every day you got to meet a president, and I didn't want the opportunity to pass me by without talking to him. I had about a million questions. At least one of them had to be worth asking.

I glanced at Virginia to see if she was going to say something. Probably not. She looked petrified.

So, I raised my hand.

"Yes, dear?" Mr. Hoover said.

I glanced at Mr. Valentine, who was eyeing me suspiciously, then looked back at Mr. Hoover.

"How come you didn't want anybody to know you were coming?" I asked. "If it were me, and I were a president, I'd want everybody to know."

"Let's just say I prefer to travel incognito these days."

"In cog, what?" I asked.

"Incognito," he repeated. "That means trying not to be recognized."

"Oh, sure. I get it," I said. "On account of some folks might not appreciate the things you done as president."

Virginia's daddy jerked upright as if he'd been stuck in the britches with a hatpin. Mr. Hoover's friend almost choked on his lunch.

"Of course, then there are the folks who love you all to pieces and would want to come out to see you, shake your hand and maybe get your autograph. Grandpa would be one of them. He said you're a saint, mostly on account of you feeding all those starving people in Europe after The Great War."

"I'd like to meet this grandfather of yours."

"Maybe in heaven," I said. "He passed away when I was ten."

Mr. Valentine cleared his throat. When I turned to look,

he raised his eyebrows like Groucho Marx.

"What?" I asked. "Did I say something wrong?"

Mr. Valentine opened his mouth but couldn't get the words out before Mr. Hoover spoke up.

"I'm sorry to hear about your grandfather's passing. I'm sure he was a fine man."

"The best."

Mr. Hoover smiled. Then he tucked the napkin in his collar and went back to the messy business of eating crawdads.

Mr. Valentine started twitching and blinking and nodding. I was mostly fluent in adult sign language. It was obvious Mr. Valentine was trying to get rid of us.

At the same time, Virginia's hand started carrying on a conversation with mine. A squeeze at first, then a pull. She wanted us to leave, too.

I didn't understand why everybody was in such a hurry for us to go. Didn't they know I had more questions?

I avoided looking at Mr. Valentine. Instead, I watched Mr. Hoover. He was a good eater. Hungry, too. He had juices flying everywhere. His napkin didn't do much to protect his starched shirt and button-on collar, nor his skinny necktie.

Come to think of it, what he was wearing didn't look much like fishing duds.

Mr. Hoover noticed me studying him.

"Is there something the matter?" he asked.

"Oh, no."

"Come, come, my dear."

"Well, you said you're going fishing?"

"That's correct."

I scratched my head.

"I'm visiting my cousin afterward. We grew up together here in Oregon," Mr. Hoover said. "I thought I'd surprise her with a stringer of fresh trout for supper."

"Well, if you're going fishing, why don't you have your fishing duds on?"

He looked at himself. "These *are* my fishing clothes."

"If you don't mind me saying so, they look more like going-to-church clothes."

He chuckled. "I can assure you these are the clothes I wear when I fish."

"You wouldn't be fooling me, now, would you? When I go fishing, I wear old, holey clothes."

He held up three fingers. "Scout's honor. Besides, you could say fishing is a religious experience to those of us who truly enjoy it. A sanctuary of sorts." He smiled, then went back to eating.

Mr. Valentine started fidgeting again. When Virginia and I looked up, he nodded toward the door, indicating it was time for us to leave. Then he cleared his throat to get Mr. Hoover's attention.

"Time to go, young ladies," Mr. Valentine said. "Please thank Mr. Hoover for his time and say goodbye."

"Goodbye," Mr. Hoover said cheerily before either of us could open our mouths. "It's been a pleasure meeting you both."

Virginia waved.

"Goodbye," I said.

I was floating on air as we left. Who would believe it? I had talked to President Hoover. In person.

"Ruby Ryan."

Mr. Hoover's words stopped me cold. Did I do something wrong?

I spun around. "Yes, sir?" I said, my face redder than ever.

"No need for concern," he said, obviously aware of my discomfort. "Mr. Valentine told me you were the one who caught these tasty crawfish. They are the finest I've ever eaten, and I mean that from the bottom of my heart. I just wanted to say thank you, Ruby."

I smiled so hard my face hurt. A president of the United States said thank you to me, little ol' Ruby Mae Ryan.

"You're welcome, Mr. Hoover," I said. I gave him my very best curtsy, at least the best I could muster in overall shorts.

Chapter 22

TROUBLE AT THE RIVER

Yesterday was a scorcher. Ninety-five degrees. It was going to be even hotter today. So when Virginia suggested spending the day at the river, I could hardly contain my excitement.

The swimming hole down by the bridge was the best spot. Folks came from all around to spend hot summer days there.

"This side of the river or the other side?" Virginia asked as we approached the bridge.

"The other side," I said. "It'll be less crowded."

We crossed over and slid down the steep embankment to the river. Nobody else was there.

"Good call," said Virginia's little sister, Emeline. "We can have any spot we want."

I preferred someplace with at least partial sun, so I sprinted ahead to stake my claim. If I left it to Virginia, we'd end up in the shade, since that's what her momma would tell her to do.

Mrs. Valentine constantly worried about Virginia and Emeline getting too much sun. I'm not sure why. They were rarely outside, and when they were they didn't get sunburned to a crisp after only twenty minutes in the sun, like me.

I spread my towel on a patch of grass and sat down. The

sun filtered through the branches of cottonwood and alder trees, casting a dappled pattern of sunlight and shadows on the ground. It was an ideal spot.

Virginia and Emeline stopped in front of me, their shadows blocking my sun.

"What's the matter?" I asked, knowing full well the answer.

"This is the best you can do?" Virginia asked.

I looked around. "What do you mean? It's perfect."

"Hardly."

"Well, where were you thinking?"

Virginia pointed to a patch of shade beneath a stand of fir trees. Not a ray of sunlight penetrated the thick boughs.

"How about if we split it?" I offered. "We can spend the first half of the day here, then move over there when we're ready to eat lunch."

"Great," Emeline said. "I'm hungry now. Let's move."

Virginia elbowed Emeline. "Yes, I think that's a fair compromise."

Virginia spread her towel beside mine. Emeline remained standing, but only long enough to let us know she was staying under protest. She finally spread her towel on the other side of me.

"Doesn't the water look delicious," Virginia said dreamily.

I had never thought of the river as delicious—more like hypnotic—but I knew what she meant. The water was calling me.

I kicked off my shoes and dashed into the river.

Virginia and Emeline were still sitting on their towels, fiddling with their shoes. They dumped out rocks and sand and arranged the shoes just so under the towels to keep the sun from fading their color.

"Don't take all day!" I hollered.

"Coming," Virginia said as she stepped gingerly on the rocky ground. "Oh, this feels lovely," she gushed when she reached the water.

Emeline was right behind her. She playfully splashed Virginia and me. "Want to see me swim across the river and back without stopping?"

"Oh, Emeline," Virginia said. "Don't be a show-off."

"I'd like to see that," I said.

Emeline did a shallow dive and glided underwater like a dolphin. Halfway across, she resurfaced and gracefully swam arm over arm to the far bank. Then, without so much as stopping, she tumbled in the water, disappearing briefly, then reappeared as she swam back toward us.

"Boy, I wish I could learn to swim like that," I said. "Emeline looked like the girl on our bathing suits when she dove in."

Virginia nodded. She examined the girl stitched on the hip of her bathing suit. "Thank you again, Ruby," she said. "This bathing suit is swell. I hope you thanked your sister for me."

The bathing suits were all the rage, though a lot of folks couldn't afford them. That included me. The only reason I had one was because Patsy sent it to me, along with one for Virginia.

Patsy worked for the company that made the suits. She was an assistant to the designer. Patsy only paid half price since they were what she called "seconds." That meant they had flaws, though neither Momma nor I could find any.

Emeline stood up and wiped the water from her face. "I adore your bathing suits," she said. "They look even more beautiful from underwater. The red is so bright."

I had to admit: We did look good. Virginia almost filled out her suit. I was getting there, but you just couldn't tell that by looking.

At first, I had decided not to wear the suit. It made me self-conscious. I didn't want people to think I was trying to be like the models in the advertisements. I was just going to wear what I had on when I got to Virginia's house—shorts and shirt—since they needed to be washed anyway.

Mrs. Valentine convinced me otherwise. She said it was okay for me to get in touch with my feminine side once in a while. Whatever that meant.

"Well, look at you!" hollered someone on the Crossroads side of the river. It was Mary Belle. She stood in the shallows with two of her friends.

I didn't know whether she was being nice or trying to start something. Virginia would tell me to give her the benefit of the doubt. So I kept my mouth shut.

"Don't you look gorgeous in those fancy red suits!" she shouted. "Why doesn't the munchkin have one to match?"

I guess that made it clear she wasn't being nice.

"We didn't come here to get into a spat with you, Mary Belle!" I shouted back.

"Me? I'm just trying to be sociable!"

By now, everyone at the swimming hole was listening to our conversation and staring. It was precisely the kind of unwanted attention I had feared.

Mary Belle whispered something to her friends. Whatever she said, it made them laugh.

"Of course, they would look a lot better if they were on someone who could fill them out!" Mary Belle teased.

Not just her friends laughed at that remark.

I knew Mary Belle was talking about scrawny me. My face turned red, which made everybody laugh even harder.

"Oh, yeah!" yelled Emeline, her fury catching me by surprise. "Well, maybe this munchkin ought to come over there and outfit you with a house, you wicked old witch!"

"Emeline!" Virginia snapped, grabbing her sister's arm. But Emeline wasn't about to back down. She pulled her arm away.

"Ruby may not have filled out yet," Emeline said,

embarrassing me to no end, "but at least she doesn't look like a circus bear wearing a tutu!"

It was Mary Belle's turn to be laughed at. Even her friends joined in.

"Don't be saying things like that," Virginia said, trying not to laugh.

Mary Belle glared at her friends until they stopped laughing. "That's tough talk for a pipsqueak!" she said. "Why don't you come over here and say it?"

Emeline waved her off. "You're not worth the trouble!" she hollered, turning and walking to her towel.

Eventually, Mary Belle and her friends went back and sat on their towels. Every now and again, we caught them giving us dirty looks and pointing, but at least they left us alone.

There had only been about a dozen kids at the swimming hole when we first arrived, but more and more showed up as the day got hotter. By noon, there were thirty or forty kids and a few adults.

Emeline sat up. "Anybody else hungry?" she asked.

"You're always hungry," Virginia said. "Mother told me supper would be late tonight, so we probably should wait to eat lunch."

"But I'm starving."

"Oh, pshaw!"

"I'm getting hungry, too," I confessed.

"See!"

"Oh, be quiet, Emeline," Virginia said, glaring at her. Virginia shaded her eyes with her arm and turned to me. "Can you wait a while, or would you really rather eat now?"

"How 'bout we do both," I said, trying to break the stale-mate. "We can kill some time, plus knock the edge off Emeline's hunger by snacking on berries. What do you say?"

"I don't think we have any berries," Emeline said.

"But we have fruit salad," Virginia said.

"I know," I said. "I'd rather have berries."

"What? You don't like my mother's fruit salad?"

Emeline giggled.

"Sometimes I do."

"Why not this time?"

"There's cantaloupe in it."

Virginia wrinkled her nose. "Oh. You're right. That doesn't sound good."

"So, where do we get berries? I thought it was too early for blackberries," Emeline said.

I smiled and leaned toward her. "Mr. Flanagan's strawberry field," I whispered.

Virginia took a deep breath. "I don't know," she said. "What if we get caught?"

"We won't. Not as long as we're careful."

"I still don't like it. We could get in big trouble."

"Look," I said, changing tactics. "Think of it as doing Mr. Flanagan a favor."

"How's that?"

"Marty said they don't pick for two more days."

"So?"

"So if the berries are ripe today, most likely they will be rotten by the time they pick again, and they'll go to waste. You ever see really nasty, rotten berries?"

"Yuck!" Emeline gagged, making a face.

"Exactly. So, how about it?"

"I'm in," Emeline said.

Virginia wasn't so sure. She studied our faces.

Emeline nodded, trying to coax her sister to say yes. She kept nodding until Virginia answered.

"Oh, okay."

"Yippee!" Emeline yelped.

Mr. Flanagan's strawberry field was only a short distance from the river. But a mountain of briars stood between here and there. Luckily, I knew a shortcut through the thicket.

"Stay down," I said when we got close to the berry field.

We crouched as we ran across open areas, using thickets here and there as cover. Our objective was to get to the corner of the broken-down fence that bordered the field.

Once we reached it, I took a quick look around. "The coast is clear," I said. "Let's go!"

I jumped a sagging section of barbed wire and sprinted to the nearest row of strawberry plants.

"Wait for us," whispered Virginia as she and Emeline followed. They looked scared out of their wits. Obviously, they had never raided anybody's strawberry patch before. Come to think of it, neither had I.

"Let's pick a few and go," I said.

"Fine by me," Emeline agreed. "I'm too young to go to prison."

We all giggled.

Emeline's remark seemed to ease the tension. She and Virginia relaxed and started picking and eating strawberries by the handfuls.

We stayed longer than we intended. We couldn't help it. The berries were super sweet and flavorful.

"Oh, no!" Emeline mumbled, almost choking on a mouthful of strawberries.

Virginia froze. "What?"

Emeline pointed to the house on the far side of the field.

Someone was coming. It was too far to make out who it was, but we weren't going to stick around to find out.

"Let's get out of here," I said.

We scattered like mice caught pilfering a feed sack. Virginia and I went one way while Emeline took off in another direction.

The three of us finally ended up back at the river, out of breath. Emeline and I were giggling on account of our little adventure. Not Virginia, though.

"I'm never doing that again," she said. Her cheeks were flushed from running but not nearly as red as the strawberry stains around her mouth.

"I thought it was fun," Emeline said, laughing.

"You see," Virginia said, her eyes fixed on me, "you've turned my sister into a juvenile delinquent."

"I think I had help from her big sister."

Virginia looked offended. Then, suddenly, she busted out laughing.

We followed the river back to our things.

"So, what's for lunch—besides your momma's fruit salad?" I asked as we came within view of the swimming hole.

Virginia rattled off the lunch menu. "Egg salad sandwiches, carrot sticks, and oatmeal cookies."

"Sounds delicious."

We sat down, and Virginia flipped open the picnic basket.

"Hey!" she exclaimed.

"What?"

"Someone—or something—has eaten most of our lunch."

"You mean like a bear?" Emeline said, gulping. She looked around.

"Would a bear wipe its mouth?" I asked, holding up a used napkin.

Virginia looked at me with wide eyes. "Why would somebody do that?"

"The only thing left is the fruit salad and carrots," Emeline reported. "Not nearly enough for the three of us."

"You can have my share of the fruit salad," I said.

"Are you sure?" Virginia asked.

I nodded.

While Virginia and Emeline ate fruit salad, I nibbled a carrot. I pondered who might have eaten the sandwiches and cookies. I didn't have to think too hard. I was pretty sure I knew who did it. The question was, what should we do about it?

Chapter 23

DIRTY TRICKS DON'T PAY

Emeline finished off half of the fruit salad in a jiffy, then wiped her mouth with one of the unused napkins. "What about our stolen lunch?" she asked.

"Not much we can do about it now," Virginia said. "The damage is done."

That made me bristle. "I'm with Emeline. I think a little payback is in order."

"That's not what she said."

"No, but I'm sure that's what she meant."

Emeline nodded.

"Proper young ladies don't get payback. What's to be gained by that?" Virginia asked. She sounded like her momma.

"What? We're going to let them get away with it?"

Virginia frowned. "We don't even know who did it. Besides, mean acts like this have a way of catching up with the guilty party."

"I have a pretty good idea who did it," I said.

"You do? Who?"

"Mary Belle Baxter."

"Oooh. I can believe it," Emeline said with a mouth full of

fruit salad. "She's a mean one."

"I can't believe what I'm hearing," Virginia said. "Let's learn from the experience and move on. Maybe next time, we won't leave our things unattended."

It was classic Virginia, always giving people the benefit of the doubt. That's not a bad thing unless, of course, your stomach is growling and someone ate your lunch. Me, I felt like crossing the river and putting a crawdad down the back of Mary Belle's bathing suit.

Of course, Virginia was probably right. Getting even with Mary Belle would only make things worse and probably get us in trouble.

We packed up our things and headed back to Virginia's house.

As we walked across the bridge, I noticed Mary Belle's two friends were getting ready to leave. They had picked up their belongings, including Mary Belle's towels and tote. Mary Belle was nowhere in sight.

That seemed odd. I scanned both banks of the river. I even looked behind us to make sure Mary Belle wasn't sneaking up on us or something.

"Why do you suppose Rene and the other girl grabbed Mary Belle's things?" I asked Virginia.

"What do you mean?"

"I don't see Mary Belle anywhere. The two girls who were with her picked up her things. Why wouldn't Mary Belle do it herself?"

Before Virginia could answer, there was a commotion at the outhouse next to the parking area.

"Come on!" a girl yelled. "Give somebody else a turn."

A long line of kids waited outside the outhouse. None of them looked happy.

"Did anybody try the door?" shouted someone at the back

of the line. "The wind could have blown the sign over to 'occupied.'"

"I'm in here!" growled a voice inside.

"What do you suppose that's all about?" Virginia asked.

"I don't know," I said.

Mary Belle's friend Rene stomped over to the outhouse and pounded on the back of the tiny, clapboard building. "Come on, Mary Belle, let's go!" she shouted. "You got a mob of people out here waiting on you!"

Mary Belle was in there?

"What was in those sandwiches?" I asked, not really expecting an answer.

Virginia shrugged. "Maybe they were out in the sun too long."

"I knew we should have set up in the shade," Emeline said.

Virginia and I gave her the "shut up" look.

"Didn't you once tell me your brother got sick on egg salad sandwiches?"

I nodded. "Sicker than a dog."

Just then, Rene brushed past us. She had her towels and tote, but had left Mary Belle's things in a pile behind the outhouse.

"What's wrong with Mary Belle?"

My question caught Rene by surprise. "Oh, hi, Ruby," she said, trying not to look at me. I could tell she was embarrassed. "Sorry about the sandwiches. Don't tell Mary Belle I said anything."

"She's the one who ate our sandwiches?"

"Sure did. All three of them. The oatmeal cookies, too. She gave Betty and me a couple carrot sticks."

"I knew it!" I said.

"Is she real sick?" Emeline asked, almost gleefully.

"I'll say. I didn't know a body could throw up that much."

"Ewww!" I said. "Do you think the sandwiches were bad?"

"Nah. Anybody would get sick if they ate that much as fast as she did."

"That's for sure," I said.

"Anyway, it looks like Mary Belle got what she deserved," Rene said, adjusting her load. "Well, gotta go."

After Rene left, Virginia said, "That wasn't a very nice thing for her to say about someone so sick."

"What? You don't think Mary Belle deserved it?" I asked.

"I do," Emeline said.

Virginia frowned. "Wasn't it you who said how horrible it was when Marty got sick on egg salad sandwiches? Do you really think Mary Belle deserves that?"

Emeline and I looked at each other. I'm pretty sure I saw Emeline start to smile.

"I suppose not," I lied.

"Of course not," Virginia said firmly. "What Mary Belle did was childish and stupid, but she doesn't deserve to be deathly ill because of it."

The line outside the outhouse had gotten shorter. Most people had given up and gone off to find a bush or use the bathroom at Mr. Abbott's store. But the few who remained were more impatient than ever.

"You going to be in there all day?" yelled a teenage boy at the front of the line.

A sudden, rumbling roar came from inside the outhouse. Only it wasn't a ferocious-sounding roar. More like the sound a very sick bear would make.

I nearly gagged.

"You better not be making a mess in there!" the boy yelled. He rattled the door for emphasis.

"Beat it!" Mary Belle hollered.

The boy must have recognized the voice. Like most kids, he knew better than to tangle with her. He stepped back, turned to see if anybody was watching, then left without another word.

I'd seen and heard enough. "Come on. Let's go back to your house," I said.

My stomach was queasy the rest of the afternoon. Thank goodness, by suppertime it had recovered. I was hungry. But I had to admit: I felt sorry for Mary Belle. A little. Though not enough to ruin my appetite for Mrs. Valentine's delicious supper and apple cobbler dessert.

Chapter 24

GONE FOREVER

Virginia and her momma were in Portland for a few days, so I had to find another way to spend my afternoons. I knew Henry was always up for a game of checkers. Today was no exception.

Henry and I were in the middle of our second game when Mr. Wilson pulled up at the store. He got out of his truck, clomped up the stairs at the far end of the porch, and started walking toward us.

Funny thing, I didn't see Buster. Usually, the two of them were inseparable when they came to Crossroads. The only time they weren't together was when Mr. Wilson went inside a business. Buster would sneak off and find an out-of-the-way corner when that happened, someplace he could lay down without being bothered.

Not today, though. Buster was nowhere in sight, which made me curious—and nervous. I still wasn't over the scare Buster had given me the last time I saw him.

I watched Mr. Wilson almost all the way to the door.

"You gonna stare all day or you gonna play?" Henry teased.

Before I could reply, Henry greeted Mr. Wilson.

"Hey, there, Elmer. How you been?"

Mr. Wilson nodded. "Henry," he said flatly.

Most folks would have stopped and chatted a while. Not Mr. Wilson. He opened the door and let it slam shut, the bell on top jangling.

I got up and stood on my tiptoes, craning my neck to see if Mr. Wilson had left Buster in the truck. Unfortunately, there was no way to tell from where I stood. I started to walk over to get a closer look when Henry said something that stopped me in my tracks.

"Maybe you didn't hear."

I turned around. "Hear what?"

"Buster is gone."

I walked back to Henry and sat down. "Gone? Gone where?"

Henry didn't answer right away. I could tell he was searching for the right words. "Mr. Wilson had to put Buster down."

What? Put him down? I knew what that meant. Every kid raised on a farm knew what it meant. We had all seen animals put down for one reason or another. It was just a nice way to say killed!

I suddenly got a sick feeling deep down inside, like the time a sheep butted me in the gut, and I threw up all over the poor thing. I hoped I didn't throw up now. Not here. Not in front of Henry.

"Why would he do that?" I groaned, struggling to get the words out but not let my breakfast come up with them.

Henry smoothed my hair. "He didn't have much choice," he said.

"But why?" My voice cracked. "Buster wasn't a mean dog. Not really. Oh, sure, he scared me once or twice, chased me. He must have been feeling poorly. I'm sure he didn't mean it. Even if he did, he didn't deserve to die."

"You may be right," said Henry, putting his arm around

me. "Buster was a good dog, but he wasn't himself lately. Don't know why. Don't know if he would ever be his old self. What I do know is he chased you, and he bit a boy a few days ago. Hurt him pretty bad."

Guilt welled up inside me. I felt partly to blame. If only I hadn't told Daddy. He wouldn't have gone over to Mr. Wilson's, and maybe Mr. Wilson wouldn't have killed Buster.

"It's my fault," I croaked.

"Nonsense, Ruby," Henry cooed, cocking his head, trying to look into my eyes. "You're not to blame for what happened."

I was too choked up to talk, so I just nodded.

"If anyone's at fault—and I'm not saying they are—but if that's the case, then it's the ones who teased Buster who should feel bad. Not you."

Then Henry told me a story he'd heard about a group of nameless, faceless boys who had been tormenting Buster. I'd heard a version of the same story from Marty.

"So, you see, it's not your fault," he concluded. "None of it."

Henry's words made me feel a little better. But the guilt remained.

I got up to go into the store, but Henry held my hand and wouldn't let go.

"Where you off to?" he asked.

"I'm going to see Mr. Wilson. I need to apologize."

Henry smiled. Not a happy smile, but a sad one. "I don't think that's a good idea, Ruby."

"Why not?"

"Mr. Wilson is taking this pretty hard. He loved that old dog. It broke his heart to have to do what he did. Trust me. He needs space and a little time."

I plopped back down in my chair. I didn't feel like talking anymore.

Henry must have sensed that. He didn't say anything either,

but I could feel him watching me. He put an arm around my shoulders, letting me know he was there and that it was okay if I didn't want to talk.

It helped, but at the same time, it didn't. It only increased the urge to let everything out. To tell someone all the things I was feeling. But I knew if I did that, there'd be no stopping the tears.

I got up and started down the front steps.

"Where to, now?"

"I gotta go."

I don't know if I was feeling sorrow, guilt, or a little of both. Whatever it was, it churned inside me like one-too-many green apples, and I couldn't sit still another minute. Besides, I didn't want Henry or the rest of the world to see me bust out crying and blubbering.

Chapter 25

A DAY AT THE FAIR

The past week had been awful. All I thought about was poor Buster. It was so sad to walk by Mr. Wilson's house now and not hear Buster's bark.

I would never forget what had happened to him, but I promised myself I'd try not to think about it anymore, at least not for the next few days. I was spending them with Virginia at the Thackeray Jubilee.

I'd been waiting for her at the front gate for twenty minutes. I didn't mind that she was late. I enjoyed watching folks pour into the fairgrounds like water out of a pitcher.

The Jubilee was a perfect place for people-watching. Folks came from all around. Town folks. Farm folks. Even some city folks from as far away as Portland and Eugene.

I was so busy gawking I almost didn't see Virginia come through the gate.

"Sorry I'm late," she said.

"That's okay."

"Say! I love your dress."

What Virginia really meant was, "Say! I'm so glad you wore a dress." Like I said before, I don't wear one very often. In fact,

I don't know exactly why I wore a dress today.

Virginia's dress put my faded, hand-me-down one to shame. Hers was a pretty summer dress. Soft yellow. Almost up to her knees. If we were at school, Mrs. Prescott would have asked her to go home and put on another dress, one with the hem a few inches lower.

Virginia hooked her arm in mine. "What do you want to do first?"

"Everything," I said. I just wasn't sure if I wanted to spend any money in the process.

"Me, too. But we've got to pick something. Otherwise, we'll just walk around in circles."

"That suits me fine."

Virginia rolled her eyes. "How about if we look around while you try to make up your mind?"

"Okay."

The food smells swirling around us made my lips smack. I could almost taste the popcorn, cotton candy, and those newfangled corndogs on a stick. But as much as I loved fair food, I wasn't going to be lured into buying any if I could help it.

"I don't know about you," said Virginia as we strolled down the midway, "but these wonderful smells are making me hungry."

"Not me," I fibbed.

"Well, maybe we could snack on caramel corn."

"Nah."

Virginia stopped. "Don't be such a party pooper."

I fingered the money in my pocket. I had ten pennies, a nickel, and a dime.

"I'm not," I said.

"It sure sounds like it to me. You said you were going to enjoy the day and spend some of your money. Remember?"

"I know. I know."

"Well?"

I thought about it for a minute. "I guess I've changed my mind."

Virginia shook her head.

"Please don't be mad, Virginia. I intended to. Really, I did. But now that we're here, I just don't know if I can."

"Why's that?"

I didn't have an answer.

"I know you're saving your money," Virginia said, "but it's okay to spend a little on yourself once in a while, especially as hard as you've been working."

"Maybe another time," I squeaked.

Virginia sighed. "Oh, okay."

I felt relieved she wasn't mad.

"But I am hungry. Starving, actually. I'm going to buy a bag of caramel corn. You're welcome to help me eat it."

I eyed her suspiciously.

"Don't look at me like that. I can't eat a whole bag."

"I know what you're up to, Virginia." I'm sure she thought if I ate some, I'd want more. Then I would need a soda to wash it down, which meant there'd be so much sugar in my system I'd want to play games and maybe go on a ride or two.

"What? Can't a girl be hungry?" Virginia asked, smiling. "And shouldn't her best friend help her out? You'd be doing me a favor, you know."

"I give up," I said, throwing up my hands.

We made our way to the nearest refreshment stand. Virginia bought a heaping bag of caramel corn, and we took turns eating it by the handful.

"Now, isn't this better than starving?" she asked, tossing a kernel of caramel corn in her mouth.

I nodded.

As we continued walking along the midway, our heads

swiveled from one booth to the next.

"Doesn't that look fun?" said Virginia, pointing to the boys trying to knock over metal milk bottles.

"Uh-huh."

Every midway game looked fun.

"You want to do the dart throw."

Virginia was taunting me. She knew I loved the dart throw. I was pretty good at popping the balloons and almost always won a prize.

"Nah."

We walked a little farther.

"How about the ring toss?"

"Nah."

Virginia wrinkled her nose.

"Oh, look at that," she said excitedly, pointing to the popgun booth. "How about that?"

"Nah. But you can."

She stopped. "Oh, come on, Ruby."

"You know I can't shoot worth a hoot, Virginia."

She shook her head. "That's not what I'm talking about and you know it."

"I thought we agreed it was okay if I didn't want to spend any money."

"Oh, I know. I thought maybe I could get you to change your mind," she admitted. "It's pretty boring just looking."

Neither of us said a word for a while. We quietly strolled the fairgrounds looking for an excuse to break the silence.

"I've got it!" Virginia exclaimed.

"What?"

"The Ferris wheel!"

Its shape loomed ahead of us like a giant oak tree.

"Nah."

"Ohhhhh! You're so frustrating sometimes."

I shrugged.

"Come on, Ruby," Virginia pleaded. "The Ferris wheel. It's a two-seater, and I don't want to ride by myself. What do you say? Two for the price of one."

"Oh, okay."

Virginia smiled. "Hurry! Let's get over there while it's stopped."

Virginia paid her dime, and the man held the seat steady while we sat down. When we were settled, he pulled down the steel bar and locked it across our laps.

I liked the Ferris wheel fine, but I could tell Virginia loved it. She never stopped smiling the whole time we were on it.

My favorite part was the view from the top. It was magnificent! We were so high we could see the entire fairgrounds and all the way to downtown Thackeray.

The Ferris wheel went around slow at first. Then, the man operating the ride started to increase the speed. Soon it was spinning as fast as I've ever gone on a Ferris wheel.

"Isn't this fun!" Virginia shouted, her hair swirling around her face.

"Uh-huh."

Truth be told, I was scared half to death and not just about having my dress fly over my head. The scariest part was the way Virginia rocked our seat back and forth. Our feet flew higher and higher as if we were on a swing.

I was never so glad as when it stopped.

"What do you want to do next?" Virginia asked excitedly, even before we got off the Ferris wheel. "Want to do the dunk tank? I saw it over by the barns."

Now, that sounded like something within my budget. I could watch some poor soul get dunked, and I wouldn't have to spend one red cent for the pleasure.

Chapter 26

THIS ONE'S FOR BUSTER

Mr. Abbott's dunk tank was a fair favorite. It put a little extra money in his pocket, but mainly he did it because people loved it so much.

Mr. Abbott once told me the secret of its popularity was penance, whatever that meant. Maybe it had something to do with how he paid local hooligans and politicians to sit in the chair. Folks loved to see them get dunked. As an added attraction, Mr. Abbott put ice in the water. Lots and lots of ice.

"Look. It's Donny Markinson," I said, pointing at the boy sitting six feet above the tank of ice water.

Donny was a year behind us in school. He had a reputation for being a bully. I suspect some of the kids waiting in line to pay their dimes had been his victims at one time or another.

"What happened to his face?" Virginia asked.

"He always looks like that."

"No. I mean the red marks. And there are scratches down his side."

"Oh, yeah, I see what you mean."

"Hey, Ruby!" Donny yelled, waving.

Virginia and I went around to the side so we could see

better. As we went, softballs thudded against the backstop behind the target or bounced harmlessly off the netting draped in front of Donny.

"Holy mackerel! You're wearing a dress," Donny said. "I've never seen you in a dress before."

"Ha ha! Very funny. Maybe if you came to church once in a while, you would."

From where Virginia and I stood, we had a clear view of Donny's injuries. The ones on his cheek looked like bite marks. He had some on his ankle, too. Scratches ran down his side and across his arms and legs.

"Were you in a fight with a bear or something?" I asked.

"Nah."

"Then how'd you get so beat up?"

Donny ignored my question. He was too busy sizing up the next person to start throwing.

It wasn't the first time I had seen him with injuries like that. He was always getting into mischief, and sometimes it left a mark.

Donny leaned back and put his hands behind his head as if relaxing at the river.

"You look comfortable," I said.

"You got it," he said. "This is easy money."

"Is that right?"

"Yeah. Mr. Abbott is paying me four bits. All I have to do is sit in this chair for two hours."

Maybe Donny was on to something. Twenty-five cents an hour was good money for a kid. And he wasn't even wet. Either he just started or people were lousy throws.

The balls continued to thud harmlessly at regular intervals.

"You been here long?" I asked.

"Nah. Twenty minutes, maybe."

Just then, Mr. Abbott dumped a bushel of ice in the water.

Donny sat up. "Hey! What's up?" he whined.

Mr. Abbott ignored him and headed back to his truck. Donny's eyes about popped out when Mr. Abbott returned and dumped a second bushel of ice in the water.

"What's with all the ice?"

"What do you think I pay you good money for?" Mr. Abbott said. He sounded serious, but I could tell he was teasing.

"A guy could freeze to death!"

"Have you gotten wet yet? No. Don't worry. Most people can't hit the broad side of a barn," Mr. Abbott said, turning and winking at me and Virginia. "Besides, we've got to play to the crowd, give people their money's worth. They like the idea of dunking somebody in ice water."

"I do, too," Donny said, "except not when I'm the somebody who might get dunked."

"Don't worry. The water can't be much colder than forty-five or fifty degrees."

"That's it," said Donny. He started to climb out of the chair.

"Sit down!" Mr. Abbott ordered.

Donny balanced on the narrow edge of the tank, unsure whether to go or stay. He knew he wouldn't get paid if he left.

"I'm paying you to sit there for two hours, and that's just what you're going to do, young man. A deal's a deal."

Donny slumped back in the chair, scowling. He folded his arms across his chest. "Fine," he grumbled.

Virginia gave me a nudge. She was ready to move on.

"We'll see you," I said, walking away. But then I stopped and turned around. "By the way, you never did say how you got scratched up."

"Oh, these?" he said, twisting his head to see the scratches along his rib cage. "That crazy dog, Buster, did it."

"Buster?" I asked. "Mr. Wilson's Buster?"

"Yeah. He attacked me."

That lit a fire in my gut. "So, you're the one!"

"If you mean I'm the one that got bit, then, yeah, I'm the one."

I stomped back to the tank and grabbed onto the netting, pushing my face into it to get as close to Donny as I could. "Did you hear Mr. Wilson put Buster down?" I hissed.

"Nope," he said. He was only half-listening, watching a kid wind up and throw.

The ball thudded against the backstop.

"Well, he did. Buster is dead!"

Donny's head snapped around. "Serves him right, that dumb dog. He bit me, you know. Not the other way around."

I about ripped my way through the netting. "He's not a dumb dog!" I yelled. I could feel the fire in my gut rush to my chest and face.

"Geez! What's your problem?"

"You're my problem, Donny. Buster is dead. And it's because of you."

"Yeah, right."

"I heard about some boys teasing him. Making him mean."

"I don't know what you're talking about."

"Sure, you do. Like ambushing Buster with slingshots, and then running to the creek and escaping on inner tubes."

Donny snickered. "Oh, yeah. That was funny. Buster jumped in the creek and tried to get us, but he couldn't swim fast enough. What a dumb dog."

"You're awful, Donny!"

"Same to you, Ruby. Now, get lost." Donny turned his back to me. "Did you hear me?" he asked without looking my way. "Go away. I'm working."

"Come on, Ruby. Let's go," Virginia whispered, grabbing my hand.

I pulled out of her grip and spun around, glaring. There was so much anger my face must have been a sight. I suddenly felt ashamed and started walking.

"Are you okay?"

"No, I'm not," I said, shaking with rage. "Donny is one of the boys who got Buster killed."

It was a terrible thing to say, but at that moment I knew it was true. That's why Buster started chasing people and why he bit Donny. Buster had never done anything like that before.

"Tell me again: Who's Buster?"

"Mr. Wilson's dog. You know, the one I told you about. The dog that chased me."

"Oh, yeah. That Buster."

"Mr. Wilson had to put him down because of what he did to Donny."

"How terrible."

"I'll say. Worse yet, Donny doesn't care one bit!"

Virginia put her arm around my neck. "Come on. I'll buy you a cherry cola."

But I wasn't thirsty. I was mad.

"Thanks, but no thanks, Virginia. I've got a better idea."

I grabbed her hand, and we walked back to the dunk tank and got in line.

"What are you doing?"

"I'm going to turn Donny into an ice pop."

Virginia was flabbergasted. "I thought you didn't want to spend any money."

"I changed my mind."

"Whatever happened to saving every penny for your you-know-what?"

"This is more important."

We must have stood in line for ten minutes. It was painful to watch the kids in front of us. None of them came close to hitting the target.

It was finally my turn.

"Well, well, if it ain't Ruby Ryan—again," Donny said. He looked more relaxed than ever. "Going to give it a go, Miss High-and-Mighty?"

I was about to say something when Virginia beat me to it.

"You might want to keep your mouth shut so you don't swallow too much water," she said.

Where did that come from? It was so unlike Virginia to say something like that. Maybe she *had* learned a thing or two from me.

"Talk is cheap," Donny said, grinning.

"All right, all right. Knock it off," Mr. Abbott said. "How many throws do you want, Ruby?"

I emptied my pocket on the table and counted the ten pennies into Mr. Abbott's hand. He put five softballs in front of me.

I wound up and threw the first ball with all my might. It sizzled straight at Donny. He flinched, closing his eyes and putting up his hands. The ball hit the net right in front of him.

"Whoa!" groaned the crowd.

Donny straightened. "Ha!" he scoffed. "You can't even throw straight. The target is over there."

While Donny laughed and made fun of me, I threw the next four balls just as hard as I could. None of them came any closer to the target than the first one.

"Come on, Ruby, you can do it!" yelled someone behind me.

"Yeah! Drop him in the water!" shouted another.

I gave Mr. Abbott my dime. He gave me five more balls. Unfortunately, all but two of them missed by a mile.

I was so disappointed, mostly because I had missed all ten times, but also because I had spent twenty cents with nothing to show for it.

"Don't give up, Ruby!" someone in the crowd yelled.

"Yeah, Ruby, don't stop," taunted Donny. "If you keep this up, I might get a bonus for all the money I'm making for Mr. Abbott."

I looked around. The crowd had gotten bigger. How could I let them down? How could I let Buster down? The problem was, I only had a nickel left.

"Ruby," Virginia said tenderly. It broke the spell I was under. "You've done your best."

Mr. Abbott leaned toward me. "Your friend is right," he whispered.

I turned and looked at the faces in the crowd again. I knew they wanted me to keep going. I could feel it. I wanted to keep going, too.

A boy behind me nodded his head. "You can do it," he said.

Donny suddenly stood up on the chair and started clowning around, taunting me. I was beginning to understand why so many people were hoping to see him get dunked.

"Spend all the money you want, Ruby. You'll never dunk me."

"Pipe down!" Mr. Abbott growled. "And sit down before you break your neck."

I had done all I could. Now, it was someone else's turn to try. I was just about to leave when Virginia put her hand in mine. But it wasn't just her hand. She had something in it, and she was giving it to me. When I realized what it was, I gave her a knowing look and nod.

She smiled.

I slapped down Virginia's nickel next to mine.

"The little lady is going to give it five more tries!" shouted Mr. Abbott.

The crowd erupted. They cheered and howled and shouted, "Dunk Donny! Dunk Donny!" over and over. It was so loud I could barely hear Virginia wish me luck.

"Are you ready?" Mr. Abbott asked.

I nodded.

He leaned over and whispered, "Maybe slow it down a bit. Accuracy. That's the ticket."

I smiled and slid the money across the counter. Mr. Abbott gave me five more balls.

I did just as he suggested. Instead of throwing it as hard as I could, I concentrated on just hitting the bull's-eye.

It worked! The first throw nicked the target. An inch to the left, and Donny would have been sipping ice water.

The crowd gasped.

"One more, just like that," someone hollered.

Donny's smug look disappeared. He sat up straight. For the first time, I saw fear in his eyes.

I threw the second ball the same way as the first. Only this time, it flew straight and true.

Clank! Splash! The chair was empty in an instant, a geyser of water raining down on it.

The crowd cheered!

Donny came up spitting and shivering. I never saw anyone pop out of the water so fast. He scrambled back into the chair and hugged his body, trying to warm himself.

Everyone was making such a ruckus that it was hard to hear what they were yelling. I heard my name and Donny's name, but that's all I could make out until the cheering faded.

"Do it again!" someone shouted.

I was too embarrassed to turn around to see who had yelled it. My face felt hot. Not in a bad way, either. In fact, I felt proud. I had done it. I'd knocked that hooligan off his perch.

I started to leave.

Virginia grabbed my elbow. "You still have three more tries," she said.

It didn't matter anymore. I had done what I'd come to do.

I turned to the boy next in line. "You can have my last three balls."

His eyes got big. "Really? Gee, thanks!"

Walking away from that wild scene was like a stroll in the clouds. I felt wonderful. The anger inside me just minutes earlier had vanished. Nothing could make me feel any better than I did at that moment.

Clank! Splash!

The crowd cheered again.

Hmm? Maybe I was wrong. The sound of Donny getting dunked a second time was even better than the first.

Chapter 27

ATTENTION HOG

On the last day of the Jubilee, I finally convinced Virginia to tour the livestock barns. We had watched animals being shown in the ring, but we hadn't seen them up close yet.

We started with the swine building. Most of the pens had just been cleaned that morning, so I figured Virginia wouldn't be so squeamish.

"Just watch out for fresh piles," I warned.

"For what?"

"You know, piles. Like that one in front of you."

I thought she was going to faint.

"You said they were trained."

"They are—to put their head up, walk, and turn—not to use the outhouse."

We turned down the center aisle of the barn. There were swine of every kind on both sides. We stopped at a couple of the pens, and I asked if we could pet their hogs or the smaller pigs. Of course, they said yes. Most kids were proud of their animals and enjoyed sharing them with folks.

"Come on, Virginia, pet this one."

She looked apprehensive. No surprise, I suppose. She wasn't

much of an animal person. Heck, she didn't even have a cat or a dog.

"Pet it," I urged.

"Does it bite?"

"Of course not. She's a real sweetie," I said, scratching the hog around the ears. "See for yourself."

"Maybe later."

So we continued down the aisle. I wanted to find a hog so sweet or cute that Virginia couldn't resist petting it.

"You're right," she said. "It doesn't smell too bad in here. Only a little."

"See. Told you."

Suddenly, Virginia stopped, a funny look on her face. She lowered her head and turned toward me.

I lowered my head next to hers and whispered, "What is it? Did you step in something?"

"Isn't that your beau over there?" she whispered.

"My what?"

"Paul Johnson. There, down the aisle."

I looked up.

"Don't! He'll see you."

"I could care less who sees me looking, especially him," I said. "If I didn't know better, I'd say you were the one who likes Paul."

Virginia didn't deny it, but she didn't confirm it either. "Don't be silly," is all she said, straightening up.

"I'm serious. You keep pointing him out, saying he likes me."

"Well, he does."

"What? Because he punched me in the shoulder?"

"That, and other things."

"Well, if he so much as thinks about punching me again, I'll knock his block off," I said, working myself into a fit. "Come on."

By the time we got to where Paul had been standing a few minutes ago, he was gone. That suited me fine.

But then, suddenly, he reappeared from around the corner toting two pails of water.

"Oh, hello, Paul," Virginia said, catching him off guard.

"Ah, hello."

"You remember Ruby, don't you?"

He nodded, setting the pails down. "Uh-huh. Sure."

Virginia nudged me in the ribs, trying to get me to join the conversation.

"Nice hog," I said.

Virginia frowned.

"Thanks," Paul said, looking puzzled.

"What's its name?" Virginia asked.

"Who? Oh, her. She's Ophelia."

"That's an interesting name," Virginia said. "I've never heard of an animal named Ophelia."

"Momma loves Shakespeare. The name comes from one of his plays."

"I suppose she has a brother called Hamlet," I joked. "Get it? Ham-let."

"How'd you know?"

My jaw dropped, though I shouldn't have been surprised. After all, Daddy's hog was named Hamlet.

"Well, not her brother, exactly," Paul said, patting and rubbing Ophelia, "but her father was named Hamlet. He was a big ol' boy."

I must have struck a chord because Paul couldn't stop talking after that. He told us all about Ophelia and how she was the prettiest piglet he'd ever seen. That came as a big surprise, he said, because her daddy, Hamlet, was the ugliest hog ever. He wondered how Hamlet could have sired such a beautiful, perfect little thing.

I loved Paul's story about Ophelia. It was so sweet. The only problem was, he didn't have much to say after he finished the story. And neither did we.

The silence was awkward.

"You think Ophelia will win first prize?" I finally asked.

"Puh! Without a doubt," he said, scratching Ophelia's head. "Come watch us in the finals this afternoon. You'll see."

"I don't know. We've still got a lot of other things we want to see."

"I'm sure we can find time," Virginia said. "Don't you think, Ruby?"

"Yeah. Come on, Ruby," Paul said. And with that, he punched me in the shoulder. Again!

Until that moment, I was going to say yes. Now, I was ready to haul off and slug him back.

Virginia read my mind. She grabbed my hand and tried to get me to walk away. But it was too late for that. I wasn't budging. Not until I had my say.

"I would rather kiss a hog than watch you showing off in the ring," I said adamantly.

Paul thought I was joking. "Ha! That's a good one," he said, slapping his leg and laughing.

Virginia raised her eyebrows and shook her head. She knew I wasn't kidding.

I took Paul's laugh as a dare. So I leaned over, put my hands on both sides of Ophelia's face and gave her a kiss, right on the snout. Or, should I say, Ophelia gave me a big, snotty kiss right on my mouth.

I straightened back up, smiling.

Paul was stunned.

Virginia looked on the verge of fainting.

"Come on," I said, grabbing Virginia's arm. "Let's go."

I had to practically drag her. She kept shaking her head in

disbelief. I led her stumbling and weaving through the barn and into the fresh air outside.

As soon as we rounded the corner, I spit. I wiped my mouth with the back of my hand and glanced behind us to make sure Paul hadn't followed. Then, I spit again. But I couldn't get the taste of hog snot out of my mouth.

"You kissed a pig," Virginia said, still dazed.

I spit again. "Actually, she's a hog. Pigs are smaller."

"You really kissed it. I can't believe you did that."

"I can't believe it, either."

"You want something to drink?" Virginia asked.

"Absolutely. I'll buy," I said, trying not to swallow.

Virginia looked surprised.

"I know what you're thinking," I said. "Let's just say I realized for the second time this week that some things are more important than saving money."

Chapter 28

THE BIG ANNOUNCEMENT

Momma's face was a dead giveaway when she was mad. Like now. It was stormy red. Her mouth was drawn tight, her jaw clenched.

The sour face was on account of company coming. Don't get me wrong, Momma loved company. The problem was she didn't know folks were coming until an hour ago when Daddy told her at supper. So now, Momma and I were making refreshments as fast as we could because people would be arriving any minute.

"I don't know why anybody would bother to tell me," Momma said to herself as she cubed apples. "After all, I'm only the one expected to clean and freshen up the place and prepare food for a house full of people."

I guess she forgot about me. I had already swept the front porch and straightened the front room. And wasn't I there, now, helping her make refreshments?

I understood why Momma was mad. What I didn't understand was why she was mad at Daddy. It wasn't his fault. He didn't know about the co-op board meeting until just before he told her. Mr. Abbott had come by with a roll of fencing—and

Mrs. Prescott, who was chairwoman of the board—and that's when Daddy found out.

"Would you be so kind as to host the meeting at your house tonight, James?" Mrs. Prescott had asked.

Daddy looked like he'd swallowed a bug.

The co-op office was too small for gatherings, so this month's meeting was supposed to be at Mr. Hanson's house. Unfortunately, Mr. Hanson fell out of a tree, broke his arm, and was getting a cast at the hospital in Thackeray.

"I would have had it at my house if it weren't for the wiring messes everywhere," Mrs. Prescott said. "I do apologize for the short notice."

I could see the gears turning in Daddy's head. He knew no matter how he answered, it would make somebody unhappy.

"Certainly," Daddy said, finally.

Mrs. Prescott smiled. "Thank you, James. I knew I could count on you."

She and Mr. Abbott left and continued up the valley. He was delivering more orders, and she—like a modern-day Paul Revere—was letting folks know the meeting location had changed to our house.

"Ruby, would you whip the cream, please?" Momma asked. "There's a new bottle of vanilla in the cupboard."

"Yes, Momma."

Momma was making her famous fruit salad. It was a favorite at church picnics and family reunions. Everybody said it was the best in the county, which was saying a lot since most folks had their own special fruit salad recipes.

We combined the fruit and whipped cream in Momma's fine crystal bowl. It was another hand-me-down from her momma. Thank goodness it was in a cupboard the day the bobcat got loose in the kitchen.

Daddy told Momma to expect at least twenty people, so

she had me put out every plate and soup bowl in the house.

When Momma finished the fruit salad, she put it in the middle of the dining room table. It was surrounded by plates and bowls, silverware, glasses, two pitchers of apple cider, and a platter heaped with cookies.

Not more than a minute later, the first of the visitors knocked at the front door. I heard Daddy greeting them.

"Is it all right if I grab a cookie and go sit down?" I asked.

"For the meeting? Are you sure you want to do that?"

"Yes, ma'am. It should be interesting."

Momma gave me a funny look.

"I'll sneak out if I get bored."

I didn't mention Daddy had told me there would be a big announcement of some kind. That's the real reason I wanted to attend the meeting.

"You can have one cookie," Momma said. "There has to be enough to go around."

"Yes, ma'am."

Just then, a man wandered into the dining room.

"Hey there, Margaret."

"Why, hello, Howard!" Momma said in her cheery, company voice.

"Your husband said there were refreshments. Your fruit salad, I hope."

"Yes, right here," she said, turning and gesturing to the table. "Help yourself."

I figured that was my cue to leave. That, or get caught up in the endless small talk as more and more people showed up.

The front room was stuffed with a hodgepodge of chairs, stools, benches, and a sofa. I decided to sit in the corner by the radio. I would be hidden, but I'd still be able to hear everything.

The corner smelled like warm, aged wood. It was my favorite spot. I liked to sit there when we listened to the radio after supper. Momma even let me leave a seat cushion on the hardwood floor to sit on.

Folks continued to dribble in until just before the meeting started. Then a whole passel showed up all at once. While they went for refreshments, Daddy looked for more chairs.

Mrs. Prescott, Daddy, and the five other board members sat at the front of the crowded room. The last time I'd seen so many neighbors in our house was after Grandpa's funeral.

Mrs. Prescott usually did most of the talking. Not at this meeting. Mr. Richardson was there to give a progress report on the power line. He was the big-shot engineer: a tall, thin man with glasses. The first time I saw him was the day Virginia and I did the lemonade run.

Daddy called Mr. Richardson a one-man show because he knew so much about power lines. He had built lines for electric companies all over the Northwest. He even worked on Bonneville Dam on the Columbia River.

He was quite a talker. Not necessarily in a good way, either. He had a flat, lifeless voice that could make a bear hibernate in summer.

I tried to be a good listener, just the same. I did okay for the first twenty minutes. I was all ears as Mr. Richardson talked about poles and wires and rights-of-way. Of course, I couldn't make heads or tails of most of what he said.

Pretty soon, my eyes glazed over and I dozed off. I must have slept a good, long while, until I was startled awake by a familiar, booming voice.

"In addition to spicy Cajun crawfish, I recommend selections of chicken and beef for those who have a taste for something more traditional."

Mr. Valentine?

I wiped the drool from the corner of my mouth and peeked over the top of the radio.

It *was* Mr. Valentine! He must have come after I'd dozed off. He stood at the head of the room, dressed in the fancy rhinestone-studded shirt and bolo tie he wore when President Hoover visited.

"I estimate a third of the attendees will eat chicken, a third beef, and a third crawfish," Mr. Valentine said. "Your members can bring their favorite potluck dishes and desserts. I will provide the main-course meats, portable stoves, cookware, serving platters, and linens. All I ask from you is a dozen or so volunteers to help with food preparation and serving."

"Splendid! I think we can we can manage that," Mrs. Prescott said.

Suddenly, everyone was talking. I had only heard part of Mr. Valentine's spiel, but whatever he said, he had the room buzzing with excitement. It must have been the big announcement Daddy told me to expect.

"Why there's one of my suppliers now," Mr. Valentine bellowed above the chatter. He gestured toward me like P.T. Barnum introducing the next act. "Ruby Ryan. She will be the crawfish supplier for your event. And let me assure you, she catches only the finest crustaceans."

Like a bright, hot light, everyone's attention turned to me.

"Well, hello, Ruby," Mrs. Prescott said. "I'm glad you could join us. In case you missed it, the co-op is having a get-together when we energize the power line next month. A picnic of sorts. Mr. Valentine is going to be the caterer."

I didn't know what to say or if I should say anything at all, so I just smiled and nodded.

"How many people do you expect to attend?" Mr. Valentine asked.

Mrs. Prescott pursed her lips and tapped them with her finger. "Hmmm? Let me think," she said, shuffling through her papers. She studied one of the sheets, then scribbled on a notepad. "I estimate two hundred forty people. That's eighty for each meat option. So, how much crawfish will we need, Pierre?"

He thought a moment. "About three hundred pounds."

I gasped! That was a mess of crawdads! I quickly estimated how much they'd be worth. Lots! More than enough to earn the rest of the money for my secret surprise.

"Is that a doable number?"

"Absolutely," Mr. Valentine said. He turned and looked at me. "Don't you agree, Ruby?"

I nodded dumbly, still stunned by the huge number.

"Good. Good," Mrs. Prescott said. "Now, let's discuss our chicken and beef needs."

They went on talking, but I didn't hear a word they said after that. I was already trying to come up with a plan to catch so many crawdads. The more I thought about it, the more reality settled in.

Most folks didn't understand the first thing about catching crawdads. It took a lot of effort. Space, too. You couldn't crowd crawdads into a holding pool and keep them there for very long. That's because they might eat each other. They'd also be easy pickings for hungry critters. So, I would only have a week to catch them—at most, eight to ten days.

I would have to use every method available—by hand, net, and traps. I'd need help, too. Lots of it. There was no other way if I was going to catch that many crawdads in such a short period.

My thoughts were interrupted when folks started clapping. Mr. Valentine had finished talking and was getting ready to leave.

"Thank you," he said, smiling and raising his arms like a politician working a crowd. "Until the big day! Goodbye, everyone!"

The room buzzed with excitement and chatter.

"Order! Order!" Mrs. Prescott shouted. "Let's move on to the next item of business."

I leaned back against the wall and sunk out of sight. The emotional ride of the big announcement left me feeling a little queasy, like the first time I rode the Big Dipper roller coaster in Portland.

As I sat there wrestling with my thoughts, I suddenly remembered what Henry had tried to tell me. Something about a legend, a place where crawdads gathered by the hundreds or more. Unfortunately, I'd only been half-listening because it sounded like another one of Henry's tall tales. But what if there really was such a place?

If it was true, I had to find it.

But first, I needed to talk to Henry.

Chapter 29

LEGEND OF CRAWDAD HAVEN

Henry was right where I thought he would be. That's because fish don't bite on hot afternoons. He was slumped in his usual chair at Mr. Abbott's store snoozing, his hat pulled down over his face.

I tiptoed up the steps and sat down beside him. He had to wake up sometime, so I figured I'd sit and wait.

"How-do, Miss Ruby," Henry said, almost as soon as I sat down. He pushed his hat back.

"Oh. Hi. I thought you were asleep."

Henry sat up. "I was."

"Sorry. I didn't mean to wake you."

"That's all right," he said, waving me no mind. "About time for a soda pop anyway. Want one?"

I shook my head. "No, thanks," I fibbed.

A cherry cola would have been swell. It had to be a hundred degrees out. But I was desperate for information, and I didn't want to take advantage of Henry twice in one afternoon.

While he was away, I tried to come up with a plan for broaching the subject of the crawdad legend without sounding desperate. After all, the first time he tried to tell me about it,

I thought it was just another one of his tall tales, and I told him so.

I figured maybe I could start with small talk and then ask him about the legend. First, though, I'd have to give him some information in trade. Something he didn't know. Sort of like a down payment.

When Henry returned, we sat awhile, watching heat waves rise off the highway. Three or four cars passed, all of them in a big hurry to get someplace else.

"So, what brings you all the way to Crossroads on a scorcher like this?" Henry asked.

Forget the small talk. I got right to the point. "Bet I know something you don't."

His eyes twinkled. "A secret, eh?"

I nodded earnestly.

He rubbed his chin. "Hmmm? What kind of secret?"

I was just about to tell Henry about Mr. Hoover's visit when I remembered the promise Virginia and I had made to him, not to tell a soul.

I fidgeted in my chair, then shrugged. "Oh, never mind."

Henry gave me a long, curious look. "This have anything to do with the president?"

How did he know that?

Henry sat with a straight face. I couldn't tell if he really knew something or if he was just a good guesser.

"President? President who?" I asked, pretending not to know what he was talking about.

"Isn't that the secret you were about to tell me?"

I looked down, watching my legs swing back and forth. Usually, I was a quick thinker, but not this time. For the life of me, I couldn't come up with a reply.

I shrugged again.

"Okay, then, let me tell you the secret," Henry said.

"President Hoover was here the other day and had a bite at the restaurant. He was on his way to the coast to do some fishing. Isn't that it, the secret you were going to tell me?"

"You didn't hear that from me."

Henry chuckled. "No, I heard it from a friend."

"Mr. Valentine?" I asked. He was the only other person who could have told Henry. Or Virginia, and I knew she would never tell.

"I heard it from the president himself."

I gasped. "You're friends with President Hoover?"

"Like this," he said, crossing his fingers.

My face puckered with doubt.

"What? You don't think presidents have friends?"

That made me giggle. "Of course, they do."

"Then, what? You don't think I have friends?"

My giggle turned into a laugh. "I know you have friends. Lots of them," I said. "Me, for one."

"Really?" he said, raising his eyebrows, teasing.

"Like this." I held up my hand and crossed my fingers the way he had done.

He chuckled.

"You really know President Hoover?"

"I sure do. He stopped by my place on his way out of Crossroads."

Henry lived in a shack along the river. Let's just say it wasn't exactly the kind of place for entertaining guests, especially not a president of the United States.

"Can't believe I never told you I fished with President Hoover once or twice. Down on the McKenzie."

"For real?"

"Yes sirree, President Hoover's quite a fisherman. I think he would rather fish than do almost anything else. I fished with President Coolidge, too."

If I were president, I'd hire Henry as a fishing guide. He was the best.

"Enough of the chitchat, young lady," he said, sitting up straight. "What's the real reason you're here? Let's have it."

I leaned on the arm of Henry's chair. "Tell me more about the crawdad legend. Please."

"You mean Crawdad Haven? Seems to me the last time I mentioned it, you laughed."

"I did? I didn't mean to. I mean, I did then, but I don't think it's a laughing matter now."

"Is that right?" Henry took a drink of cherry cola. "What would you like to know?"

"Everything."

"I see. I thought you didn't believe in that sort of thing."

"Oh, that. I thought you were funning me."

"What changed your mind?"

I shrugged. "I gotta find someplace like that. That's all. On account of I need to catch lots of crawdads, fast."

"Funny how a person can believe in something when there's no alternative," Henry said, grinning.

For a minute, I was afraid he would leave it at that. Then a strange expression came over his face as he looked up and scanned the horizon.

"It's a special gathering. Something you don't see every day," he said. "Look at me. I'm as old as a Doug fir. I've spent more of my life in the woods and on the water than I have indoors, but even I've only seen Crawdad Haven twice."

I leaned toward him, mesmerized by his words. "Really? You've seen it?"

He nodded. "The first time was when I was about your age. I was fishing for sunfish in Spring Creek in north Georgia."

"You mean Crawdad Haven is in Georgia? That doesn't do me no good."

Henry ignored my interruption.

"Another time was on a creek in Missouri. There were so many crawdads I couldn't begin to count them."

"I'm confused. How did you see it in two different places?"

Henry shook his head. "Crawdad Haven isn't a place," he said. "Not exactly. It's more like a happening, an event, so to speak. It probably happens wherever crawdads live, when conditions are right."

"I see. Have you ever seen crawdads do that around here?"

Henry shook his head. "I'm afraid not."

"Oh."

"But here's the deal. Both times I saw Crawdad Haven on a summer morning when the water levels were low to middling. Like they are now."

"Wish I could find Crawdad Haven."

"You know what they say about wishes," he said, tapping the arm of his chair for emphasis after every word. "You have to sprinkle them with hard work."

"What's that supposed to mean?"

"It means you can't wait around for the wish to come true. In this case, you have to go looking for Crawdad Haven and keep looking."

"So, you think there's really a chance?" I asked, scooting to the edge of my chair.

"I suppose. As much of a chance as not. It's just you've gotta be out there catching crawdads everywhere you can think of. Maybe you'll find it, maybe you won't. But you won't find it if you don't look. You have to believe that maybe—just maybe—you'll find it."

"I can do that. I can believe."

"I know you can," he said, tooting one of my pigtails.

"Well, that's what I'm going to do," I said, jumping out of my chair.

"Hey, there. One minute," Henry said. "Remember what we talked about. Take only as many as you need and not all from one spot."

"Oh, sure. I know."

I started down the porch steps.

"And another thing," he said before I got far, "Crawdad Haven's out there, sure enough, but don't get your hopes too high."

It was too late for that. My mind was already swimming with visions of Crawdad Haven. But that's all it would be—visions in my head—until two weeks after next when it was time to actually start catching crawdads for the picnic.

"Thanks for the advice, Henry."

"You're welcome," he said. "Good luck! If anyone can find Crawdad Haven, it's you, the Crawdad Champ."

Chapter 30

GUARD DUTY

My house was less than a hundred yards away, but Virginia and I were having ourselves a campout. We had pitched a pup tent near the campfire pit down by the creek and planned to spend the night.

But it wasn't just any old campout. We were on a mission. Virginia, Laddie, and I were there to keep raccoons and other critters from stealing crawdads from the holding pool.

The pool was a section of the creek walled off by rocks where we had been putting the crawdads for the co-op picnic. The water could get in, but the crawdads couldn't get out.

I had built a fire earlier, and Virginia and I cooked pork and beans and biscuits for supper. The biscuits were the kind you wrapped around a stick. They were toasted over the fire, then slathered with butter, sugar, and cinnamon.

As a treat, Virginia was preparing popcorn she brought from home. We borrowed Momma's long-handled frying pan and her canning pot lid to cover the pan to keep the kernels from popping into the fire.

"I hope this works," Virginia said. "I've never made popcorn on a campfire."

"I'm sure it will be delicious."

Virginia clapped the lid on the frying pan. A shower of sparks swirled in the air when she put the pan on the grill to heat.

It was already getting dark, the first stars of the evening twinkling in the northern sky.

"Have you ever slept outdoors before?"

Virginia smiled weakly. "No. This is my first time."

"Don't worry. It's not much different than sleeping indoors."

"No, I suppose not," she said, "except for maybe no roof over our heads, no walls between the wild animals and us, and no light except for the campfire."

"The tent has a roof," I said, grinning.

"Is that what you call it?"

The tent was nothing more than a worn piece of canvas draped over a ridge pole. It was held up by a forked stick on each end. The sides of the canvas were pulled taut and staked to the ground. It was barely big enough for both of us. Another piece of canvas was spread on the ground inside, with a wool blanket and a quilt on top.

"We probably don't even need a tent," I teased. "There might be dew in the morning, but it's not going to rain."

"Don't push it," Virginia said, giving me a nudge as she sat down beside me.

We watched the fire while the popcorn heated and listened to the choir of crickets chirping. There was even the distant howl of a coyote.

"Ruby?"

"Yeah?"

"Did you bring a light?"

"Sure did."

"Can we turn it on?"

I was about to ask her why when I realized she was probably

afraid of being outside in the dark. It didn't seem to matter that we were sitting in the glow of the campfire.

"Sure, I'll go get it."

"I'll come with you."

"Okay. You can help me make up our beds while we're there."

It was dark beyond the campfire light, so I took her hand to guide her. I couldn't see much, but I knew where most of the tripping hazards were.

"Let me light the lantern before we make up the beds," I said.

"I'd really like that."

I pumped the piston on Daddy's newfangled lantern, then opened the valve a crack. It started to hiss. I struck a match, stuck it up inside the globe, and there was a sudden whoosh and a ball of flame inside. In an instant, the curtain of darkness lifted around us.

"That's better," Virginia sighed.

We made up our beds by folding everything in half lengthwise. I volunteered to use the wool blanket since it was scratchy and Virginia was my guest. She got the quilt. It was soft with age and warmer than the blanket.

In the meantime, we had forgotten about the popcorn. The kernels by now were rattling against the lid like hornets trapped in a tin can.

"Better grab the popcorn before it burns," Virginia said. She picked up the lantern and hustled to the campfire.

She lifted the lid with a forked stick.

"Perfect!" I chirped.

"Not exactly," Virginia said, looking closer. "But not bad. Some of the bottom kernels got burned."

She put the pan on a large, flat rock between us. We both grabbed a handful of kernels and started popping them into our mouths.

"Mmmm! Delicious!" she said.

"See. Everything tastes better outdoors."

After a few salty handfuls, we walked down to the creek and pulled out the bottles of orange soda Virginia had brought. They were good and cold.

The fire had died down to low, purple-blue flames and glowing orange embers. We sat and watched its colorful light show as we sipped sodas and munched popcorn.

"Want to tell scary stories?" I asked.

Virginia's eyes got wide. "No. No, not really."

"How about a song?"

Virginia had a beautiful voice.

"That would be fun," she said. "What do you want to sing?"

"It doesn't matter to me. You start singing, and I'll join in."

Virginia looked at the sky, thinking. Then, as if serenading the moon, she began to sing "By the Light of the Silvery Moon."

Laddie sat up, his tail wagging.

It was unbelievable. Here was a girl afraid of the outdoors, the dark, outhouses, and so many other things, but it didn't bother her one bit to belt out a song in front of other people. Not just here, but in front of a crowd, like when she sang solo at the school Christmas program.

"Come on!" she shouted between verses, giggling, "Join in."

And so, I did.

We didn't sound half bad.

"Let's do another one," I said.

Next, we sang "Home on the Range," then the spaghetti song, and after that, a half-dozen other campfire favorites.

We rocked from side to side as we sang. We even sang out of tune once or twice to see if we could get Laddie to howl. He never did.

"My voice is getting hoarse," Virginia complained.

"Okay, then, last song. Any requests?"

"How about 'We're Off to See the Wizard'?"

"I love that song!"

Virginia and I had gone to see the movie—twice—even though the wicked witch and flying monkeys scared us half to death.

Virginia stood up and held out her elbow. "Shall we?"

I hooked my arm in hers and away we went, skipping around the campfire as we sang. We must have sung and skipped to the tune three or four times before finally collapsing to the ground, out of breath.

We were quiet for a while after that. Maybe it was because we were tired. More likely, it was because we were hypnotized by the dying embers.

"Do you really think there's such a place as Crawdad Haven?" Virginia asked.

I shrugged. "At first, I didn't. Then, I did. I don't know what to think now."

"Real or not, I think you've done incredible, working as long and hard as you have."

"Thanks, Virginia." I stirred the fire, banking the coals for the night. "Maybe that's the real Crawdad Haven."

"What do you mean?"

"Maybe the looking—and catching all the crawdads in the process—maybe that's what it's really all about."

"You might be right."

"Makes sense, anyway," I said. "We've caught an awful lot of crawdads in eight days. Way more than I thought we ever could."

"Are there enough?"

"No. We still need more. Lots more." I scanned the hundred-foot stretch of creek that was the holding pool. It sparkled in the moonlight. "We're at least a hundred pounds shy of what your daddy said we need for the picnic."

"Does that mean you're still short of money?"

I nodded.

"Well, don't worry. There are still two more days."

"Leave it to you to look on the bright side."

Virginia smiled, then leaned sideways and bumped her shoulder to mine. "That's what friends are for."

I smiled and bumped her back. "You ready for bed?"

"I thought you'd never ask."

"We'll have to stay alert for critters tonight."

"You know me; I'll be listening," Virginia said, poking fun at her fears.

We drank the rest of our sodas and cleaned up before bedding down for the night.

Virginia was sawing logs long before I dozed off. As I lay there, I wondered how much sleep we would get. Not much, probably. The critters were bound to come calling at the holding pool, and we'd have to chase them off. Maybe more than once. But let them come. We were ready.

Chapter 31

UNEXPLAINED HEAD SCRATCHERS

The side of the pup tent glowed yellow-orange. It was so bright I could almost see it through my eyelids as I started to wake. For a groggy moment, I thought I was dreaming, but then I rolled over and put my hand in the cool, dewy grass outside the tent.

Panic startled me wide awake.

"Virginia! Get up!" I shouted, throwing back my blankets and squirming out of the tent.

It was a gorgeous morning. But weather wasn't my concern. We had slept the whole night through. Either critters hadn't come, or we had snoozed right through their visit.

Fortunately, Laddie was still there. That was a good sign. He was curled up at the foot of the tent chasing squirrels in his sleep. At least he hadn't deserted us in the middle of the night.

"Virginia!" I barked again.

She moaned. "What is it?"

"Get up."

"Is it morning?"

"Yes. And we may have a problem."

Virginia was slow to crawl out of the tent. She yawned and

rubbed her eyes as she stood up and stretched.

"Come on," I urged, heading for the holding pool.

Virginia struggled to keep up.

When I reached the creek, I splashed my face with water and rubbed the sleep out of my eyes. I could see the familiar reddish-brown shapes of crawdads carpeting the bottom of the pool.

Everything looked just the way we had left it the night before. There were no telltale signs of late-night visitors, like tracks or piles of crawdad carcasses. Just the same, I wanted to take a closer look. I grabbed the window box and waded into the water, scanning the bottom of the creek as I went.

"How's it look? Did we lose any?" Virginia asked.

"Not that I can tell."

I crisscrossed the lower end of the holding pool where crawdads tended to congregate. In most places, I had to walk carefully to avoid stepping on them.

"I don't understand," I said, wading out of the creek. I dropped the window box on the bank beside Virginia. "It looks like they're all there."

"So, it worked? We kept the animals away?"

I rubbed my neck. "I suppose."

"Why the concerned look then?"

"It doesn't make any sense."

"What doesn't?"

"This. The holding pool. Nothing was disturbed."

"That's a good thing. Right?"

"Yeah, sure, but why didn't the raccoons come?"

"Maybe they were afraid of us."

"Hardly. If there were enough raccoons, two or three could keep Laddie running around in circles while the others hauled off a bunch of crawdads."

"Maybe that's what they did."

"Nah. We'd have heard the fuss."

I looked at the pool, then at Virginia.

She shrugged.

It didn't make sense. Why wouldn't critters come? That question puzzled me all through breakfast and cleanup and right up until Virginia was ready to leave.

"You got everything?" I asked.

"Uh-huh. You know I would have stayed and helped you all week, except my aunt in Eugene is feeling poorly. Mother and I are staying with her for a couple days."

"It's okay. I understand."

"I'll be back in time to help at the co-op picnic."

"I appreciate that."

Virginia gave me a hug.

"What's that for?"

"I had fun," she said, throwing her satchel over her shoulder. "Especially last night. We'll have to do it again."

"I'll make an outdoor woman out of you, yet."

"You might at that," she said. She jumped on her bicycle. "Well, so long."

"Hey, wait for me!"   .

"What?"

"I'm coming with you."

"You don't have to do that."

"No. I know I don't have to. It's just that I've got to talk to Mr. Abbott about something, so I figured I'd go to Crossroads with you."

"Sounds good to me."

"Wait right here. I've got to get something first."

I ran to the house and grabbed a project I'd been working on for awhile. It was inside a gunnysack and weighed a ton. I picked it up and ran lopsided back to where Virginia was waiting for me.

"What is that?"

"A surprise."

"Are you going to tell me what it is?"

"You'll see." I hefted the gunnysack over my shoulder, and we started for Crossroads.

We went a short distance, then Virginia stopped. She nudged me with her elbow as I caught up to her. Between that and the load I was carrying, I just about fell over.

Virginia laughed. "What have you got in there? An anvil?"

"Something like that."

"It would be easier if you tied it on my bicycle."

"No thanks."

"Why not?"

"I gotta carry it. It's part of the pact."

Virginia gave me a puzzled look. "The pact? The pact with who?"

"You'll see."

"Tell you what," Virginia said, "you carry it six more electric poles, then we'll switch and you can ride with it on my bicycle for six poles. We can swap back and forth like that until we get there—wherever *there* is."

I thought about it for a second. "Okay. Works for me."

We talked about everything under the sun as we went. The conversation made the time and the electric poles go by faster.

"Almost there," I said.

"You mean for the big reveal."

"Yup."

Good thing, too. The load was starting to wear on me. I was sweating and breathing hard, and my shoulders stung where the gunnysack had scraped off the skin.

"See that fence post," I said, pointing. "That's the start of Mr. Wilson's property. Used to be as soon as I passed it, Buster would start barking."

Sadness clouded Virginia's face. "It's too bad about Buster. What a terrible thing."

"I know."

"Does your surprise have anything to do with him?"

"Uh-huh."

When we got to Mr. Wilson's, I stopped and put the gunnysack down by the post at the side of the driveway. I reached into the sack, wrapped my arms around the object inside, and hugged it to my chest. When I stood up, the sack slipped off and fell to the ground.

"What is it?" Virginia asked, trying to get a better look. Her voice went suddenly flat. "Is that a rock?"

"Just wait. You'll see."

I placed the object against the fence post.

"There," I said, standing back to admire my creation.

"It's beautiful!" Virginia gushed, kneeling for a closer look.

She had been half right: It was a rock. A huge, flat river rock with thousands of sparkling bits of mica, feldspar, and quartz, and a big red heart painted on the front. Above the heart in black letters, it said "Buster."

"I can't begin to understand why you did it, what with Buster attacking you and all, but you obviously felt the need," Virginia said.

"I don't know exactly why, either," I said, my throat tightening. "And it's not much, but I had to do something."

Virginia stood up. "I think it's a wonderful gesture," she said, hugging me.

Chapter 32

A BRUSH WITH DEATH

I don't think Henry thought I stood much of a chance of finding Crawdad Haven. He didn't come right out and say it, but I could read between the lines.

If I didn't find it, it wouldn't be for lack of trying.

I had looked everywhere. For more than a week, I had searched the creek and its tributaries for miles and miles. The river and nearby ponds, too. I caught lots of crawdads along the way, but I never set eyes on anything like the magical place Henry described.

Time was running out. With less than two days until the picnic, all I was trying to do was catch enough crawdads to earn the rest of the money I needed for my secret surprise.

As I walked in the shallows looking for crawdads, Marty and two of his friends appeared on the far side of the creek. I'd heard them running in the woods all morning.

They were playing like boys do when they're together. Acting wild and crazy. Hootin' and hollerin', breaking what they could and throwing what they couldn't.

"Look!" yelled one of them, pointing. The boy reached down, picked up a big rock, and heaved it into the creek. An explosion of water gushed into the air.

"What is it?" Marty hollered, scanning the creek.

"An enemy submarine, sir!"

"Ahhhhh! Get it!"

Soon all the boys were throwing rocks at the imaginary danger. Bending, picking up, and throwing as fast as they could.

"Did we get it?"

"I don't know!"

Marty pointed. "Look! There's another one!"

A salvo of rocks splashed into the creek, creating watery explosions.

Then it hit me: They were throwing at crawdads.

"Hey! Stop that!" I yelled.

They must not have known I was around because they froze like statues as soon as they heard me. I had caught Marty in mid-throw, a rock frozen in his raised hand.

"Don't throw rocks at the crawdads!" I dropped my pail and stumbled across the rocky bottom toward them.

"Don't mind her," Marty said finally, and he let fly the rock in his hand.

"Hey!" I yelled again. "I said, stop it!"

"Mind your business."

"If you're doing what I think you are, then it *is* my business," I said, stopping in front of him.

"We're not hurting anybody."

"What do you call trying to smash crawdads?"

"Oh. That."

"Yeah, that."

"They're just dumb crawdads."

I scowled. "That's mean and wasteful."

"What's the difference between what we're doing and people catching and eating them? Besides, we hardly hit any."

"There's a big difference," I said, taking a step closer.

Marty shoved me. It wasn't a hard shove, but it was enough to knock me off balance. I stepped back and tripped on a rock and fell underwater.

When I came up gagging and spitting creek water, the boys were laughing.

"That does it!" I yelled, water running off my head. I raised my net, threatening Marty. "You better leave if you know what's good for you."

Quick as a snake strike, Marty grabbed my net. "Come on, guys! Run!"

The boys took off across the creek, laughing like hyenas as they churned through the water. I tried to catch them, but they had too big of a head start.

As they passed the old bridge, Marty stopped long enough to throw my net. It sailed over the mountain of briars growing on the bridge and disappeared.

"Marty!" I screamed.

It was too late. He and his buddies disappeared into the woods.

I stopped at the edge of the creek, out of breath. My feet and ankles ached from the effort. There was no time for such nonsense, I thought to myself. I had to get back to crawdad catching.

If I had another net, it might not have mattered so much. But I didn't. And there wasn't enough time for Daddy to help me make a new one. I had no choice: I had to find my net.

"Right about there," I said, extending my arm and sighting down its length to mark where my net had disappeared. I kept my arm aligned on the spot as I waded toward the bridge.

A lumber company had built the old bridge long ago and used it to haul logs out of the mountains. Nobody used it anymore. The ancient wood and dirt structure was nothing more than a bramble heap now.

The bridge formed one side of what my brothers called The Fort. The other three sides were the waterfall downstream and the thick, tangled brush walls on both sides of the creek between the bridge and waterfall. It was called The Fort because it was almost impossible to get into. The stretch of creek inside hadn't been seen in years.

If I was going to retrieve my net, the fastest way to do it was to go under the bridge. I squatted down and peered between two sets of supports. I couldn't see all the way across, but light from the other side danced and jiggled on the surface of the water, so the passage was at least partially clear.

It would be a tight fit. The water was no more than three feet deep underneath, and there was only a foot of space between the water and the bottom of the bridge. The far side of the bridge had settled in the mud and was even closer to the water than this side.

"Well, here goes nothing."

I got on my knees and worked my way slowly under the bridge. The water was cold and lapped at my shoulders. It got deeper and picked up speed as I went.

I had to cock my head to one side to avoid scraping it on the crusty underside of the bridge. Even still, my hair kept getting snagged on long slivers poking down from the rough-cut beams. The bottom of the bridge was so close I could smell it, like the stink of a hog waller, only fishier.

Eventually, the water was lapping at my ears. That's when I started to get scared.

"Halfway there," I said out loud, trying to keep my courage up. "Can't quit now."

Suddenly, the creek bottom fell out from under me. Before I could hold my breath, I was underwater and had sucked in a gut full of creek.

My fear instantly turned to panic.

I thrashed and flailed like a crawdad caught on its back, but my legs were bent and trapped underneath me. I couldn't have been underwater for more than a few seconds, but it seemed forever. Long enough to see the people and scenes of my short life riffled like a deck of cards in front of my eyes.

Somehow, I regained my bearings and righted myself. I got my feet underneath me, pushed off the bottom, and blasted out of the water into an air pocket between beams. I grabbed the bridge with both my hands and feet, clinging to it like a drowned cat scared half out of its wits.

I gasped for air, my heart racing. Then a piercing scream leaped from my throat. It was a terrifying, unnatural sound that came without thought or warning. I couldn't believe it had come from me. But it had, from somewhere down deep inside.

Being scared was nothing new. I'd been chased by a bull, almost bitten by a dog, fought bullies twice my size, and sped down Ski Jump Hill on Bill's rusty old bicycle without brakes. But I had never been so terrified as I was at that moment.

"Stay calm!" I screamed at myself.

My muscles shook with fear and exhaustion. I tried to slow my breathing, but it was hard with my heart pounding so fiercely.

I hung there a good, long while, watching the water rush by. When I couldn't hold on any longer, I unwedged my feet and let the lower part of my body dangle in the water. I hung onto the beam and used my feet to search for the bottom. I couldn't feel anything directly below me, but I found the sides of the hole I'd fallen into and straddled it on wobbly legs.

Straight ahead, a dim, green light filtered through a curtain of blackberry vines.

"Just a little farther."

Moving was more awkward now. With my legs straddled,

half-bent, I leaned back like a limbo dancer to keep my face out of the water and edged forward with baby steps. I kept one hand on a beam and the other outstretched in front of me to feel for obstacles.

It wasn't long before I ran into the first of the blackberry vines. Getting poked and scratched was never so welcome. It meant I was almost out.

I pushed the vines aside as best I could. They fought back, wrapping around my arm and latching onto my clothes. I kept pushing. With every step, it got harder and harder. Finally, the vines were so thick I couldn't go any farther.

What now? One option was to go back the way I had come. But I was exhausted and it seemed too far, and I'd have to fight the current all the way. Truth be told, I was afraid to go back. I wasn't sure I could make it.

"Think, Ruby!"

That's when I realized I hadn't felt any vines around my lower legs. Maybe they didn't go that deep. Instead of trying to push through the briars, perhaps I could go under them.

It was worth a try.

I took three deep breaths. On the last one, I held my nose and submerged. I flattened against the bottom and slithered over the creek bottom like an eel.

I had to push vines away, but there weren't as many as there had been above water. Even still, they curled around my arms as I swam. Others grabbed at my hair and clothes. But I wasn't going to let them stop me. Like a dog pulling against its leash, I swam through them with everything I had.

Gradually at first—and then all at once—the vines lost their grip, and my body surged forward. My head popped out of the water, and I gulped a big, delicious breath of air.

"I made it!" I shouted, slapping the water for emphasis.

When I stood up, my legs felt wobbly, and my strength was

totally spent. I took a few unsure steps, then sprawled across a boulder as if it were a big, warm bed. It was rough and hard, but it felt so good.

Chapter 33

JUST AS HENRY DESCRIBED

I hugged the boulder a good long while before attempting to get up. My body ached and felt heavy as lead, and I had swallowed so much water I felt sick.

Daddy would have called what I'd just been through a teachable moment. I considered it a terrifying one. Either way, it was something I'd never forget.

All I wanted to do now was find my net and get back to crawdad catching. As I looked around, I realized that wouldn't be easy.

Tangles of brush billowed all around me. I stood in an open, cave-like void, with a canopy of twisted vines overhead. Everywhere else along the bridge was clogged with impassable knots of briars and debris.

No doubt I had been lucky. I couldn't help but wonder what might have happened if I had tried to go under a different section of the bridge. There would have been no getting through.

The question now was how to get out of there.

"Well, I'm not going back the way I came," I told myself.

There had to be a way out. Maybe there was an animal trail or a spot where the brush wasn't so thick, and I could hack through. It was just a matter of finding a weak point.

But first, I had to find my net.

I waded downstream toward an opening in the brambles. It was slow going because of my wobbly legs and the jumble of slippery rocks on the creek bottom.

When I stepped out of the shadows, my eyes winced against the brightness. I tried to shade them with my arm, but it did no good. I had to turn away and close my eyes for a minute.

I stood there, letting the sun work its magic. It was hot but welcome because being submerged in the cold water under the bridge had chilled me to the bone.

When I opened my eyes again, it was still bright, though my shadow helped reduce the glare a little. It was enough so that I could vaguely see crawdads patrolling the creek bottom.

"Where did you come from?" I asked out loud.

There were half a dozen or more crawdads at my feet. It was an unusual sight. I rarely saw so many together, and it made me curious. Maybe there were more.

I looked up and squinted against the brightness. The glare off the water was intense, and the creek banks shimmered with heat waves. What I could see looked like a mirage.

Through the gauzy haze, the rocks and sand on both banks were dappled with reddish-brown shapes, as if covered with the rusty leaves of fall. But that couldn't be. It was August.

I covered my eyes with my hands and squinted through the cracks between fingers. It was a trick Henry had taught me, and it worked like a charm. Not only did it reduce the glare, but I could see everything in sharp focus.

"Oh, my gosh!"

I couldn't believe my eyes. It was like peeking through the keyhole of a room filled with treasure.

It had to be Crawdad Haven!

The scene was just as Henry described. Crawdads were

everywhere. Hundreds of them. Maybe thousands. They were thick as tourists on the beach at Coney Island I'd seen in newsreels.

I reached down and caught two of the crawdads and studied them a moment. They spread their claws, waving them, arching, trying to pinch me. I suppose if they did, at least I would know it wasn't a dream.

"There's no other explanation," I whispered to myself, certain it was Crawdad Haven. Then I shouted, "I found it!"

My words echoed along the creek and sent birds flying.

I stood there with my arms outstretched to the sky, eyes closed, feeling the sun's warmth on my face. I was enjoying my moment of triumph.

The feeling didn't last long, once I remembered what had to be done next. I still had to find a way out.

For a moment, I considered escaping by climbing down the waterfall. It wasn't very tall, only eight feet or so. But the creek ran swift and deep at the brow of the fall, and I knew the rocks would be moss-covered and slick. Even if I could get down safely, there was no way to get back up to take advantage of my find.

I decided the best approach was to work my way to shore and search for a weak spot in the wall of The Fort.

I kept to the shadows as I moved. That way, I could better see the bottom of the creek and avoid stepping on crawdads. Once on shore, I tiptoed over and around them. They were everywhere! I even saw piles of crawdad carcasses where critters had stopped to feast here and there.

Animal tracks led me to narrow tunnels through the brambles. The passageways were far too small for me to squeeze through, but they seemed as good a place as any to try to hack my way out.

A rusty metal bar lay half-buried nearby. It was the length

of a baseball bat, only heavier, with a sharp edge on one side and a hunk of metal on the end. It was perfect for the job.

Even still, hacking through the brambles was exhausting, painful work. The effort cost me more scratches, bruises, and blisters than I could count. It also took more than an hour, but eventually I managed to hack a gaping hole in the wall of The Fort.

I was elated! Not only had I escaped, but now there was a passageway big enough for me to easily return to the treasure of Crawdad Haven.

I raced the quarter-mile to the barn and returned with two pails. Within ten minutes, I had both pails filled to the brim with crawdads. Instead of dumping the crawdads in the holding pool, I kept right on walking, headed for the house. The discovery of Crawdad Haven was a big deal, and I wanted to show everyone what I had found.

The pails were heavy and bashed my legs with every step. My arms ached. I longed to set the pails down and rest, but the crawdads were crowded and agitated, and I didn't want to keep them out of water any longer than necessary.

When I got to the house, Momma was on her hands and knees scrubbing the kitchen floor. She reared up like a horse, sitting back on her heels and thrusting her fists on her hips.

"Young lady, get your dirty feet off my clean floor," she scolded.

I stood there with a big, silly grin on my face, as if I hadn't heard a word she said. I must have been a sight with all the mud, sweat, and bloody scratches.

"Look, Momma! Crawdads!"

"That's nice, honey. Now, please take them outside before I put you to work recleaning this floor."

Momma's words pricked like a needle and deflated my excitement as if it were a punctured balloon. Instantly, exhaustion washed over me, and I no longer had the strength to hold the pails and had to put them down—on Momma's clean floor.

"Ruby Mae Ryan!" she huffed.

Just then, Daddy appeared. "What's all the racket?"

"Lookie," I said, trying unsuccessfully to lift the pails.

Daddy pushed back his hat. "That's quite a haul," he said, obviously impressed.

Momma folded her arms and glared. "Excuse me," she said, getting Daddy's attention. "Your daughter seems to think it's okay to tramp across my clean floor with her dirty feet."

Daddy took off his hat and scratched his head.

"It's Crawdad Haven, Daddy!" I blurted before he could say a word.

"Excuse me?"

"Henry told me about it," I explained. "Crawdad Haven, where crawdads gather by the zillions. I found it, Daddy! See! It only took ten minutes to fill both pails."

"Is that a fact?"

I nodded and told him the whole story. Well, most of it. I left out the part about almost drowning.

Momma was paying attention, too, but not necessarily on account of the story. The more I talked, and the more Daddy listened, the redder Momma's face got.

"James!" she finally snapped.

One look at Momma, and Daddy understood her meaning.

He put his hand on my shoulder. "I'm proud of you, Ruby. You'll have to tell your mother and me more about it later," he said. "For now, how about you take those pails outside and empty 'em?"

I nodded. "Okay."

Daddy looked at Momma. Her expression hadn't changed.

"And after you do that," he continued, "I want you to clean yourself up and come back and help your mother."

"Yes, Daddy."

I picked up the pails and waddled out the back door and down to the holding pool. I tried to count the crawdads as I poured them out, but there were too many and they came out too fast.

When I was done, I stood admiring the day's catch, imagining what the holding pool would look like tomorrow. I knew it wouldn't take long to fill it with the crawdads I needed, now that I'd found Crawdad Haven. Probably no more than a couple of hours. I wouldn't even need the window box, traps, or a net to do it.

Come to think of it, I never did find my net. I suppose it doesn't matter now. Crawdad Haven would provide more than enough crawdads for Saturday—and for my wish.

Chapter 34

CELEBRATING A NEW ERA

Everyone in the valley was excited when the big day arrived—everyone but Marty. He was such a mutton head sometimes. He considered it just another day. Of course, he thought the same thing about Christmas and the Fourth of July.

I suppose Marty had a point if it were only a matter of seconds, minutes, and hours. But the first day of electricity was so much more than that.

Starting today, folks in the valley would finally have electric lights and all the marvelous things electricity made possible. It was indeed a day worth celebrating.

Our farm had been chosen for the big celebration. Grassy areas had been cut. The front of the barn had a fresh coat of red and white paint. All the farm equipment had been put away or tidied up.

Linen-covered tables, chairs, and benches filled every corner of our yard and the expanse of ground in front of the barn. Pastor Morton had even loaned Daddy some pews so there would be enough seats for everybody.

Folks started arriving early. One or two automobiles at a

time, at first, then handfuls of them all at once. Pretty soon, a line of cars and trucks backed up onto the valley road in both directions, waiting to park.

My brothers and their friends directed traffic. They sent the cars from the road down our drive, across the farmyard, and into the lower pasture.

One of the first things folks saw was the canvas billboard hanging on the barn. It was painted with trees and mountains and a house with its windows all aglow. "Alder Valley Electric Cooperative" was printed in giant, two-foot-tall letters across the billboard. Underneath in smaller letters, it added, "Built and owned by YOU."

Daddy and the other co-op board members stood together in front of the billboard, greeting everyone as they arrived. It reminded me of a wedding reception line.

Some folks found a table and sat down to listen to the Grange band, but most stood around talking with neighbors. The kids chased each other across the yard or wandered down to the creek to throw rocks.

Each family brought a favorite potluck dish and added it to the tables filled with casseroles, salads, and desserts. Two ladies stood at the tables as self-appointed food monitors. They kept kids from sneaking a taste of sweets before supper.

Meanwhile, Momma was elbow to elbow with a dozen other ladies putting the final touches on veggie dishes, cheese platters, and gallons of Momma's fruit salad. Behind them sat a dozen washtubs filled with extra food half-buried in ice chips.

Virginia and I helped Mr. Valentine baste more chicken with barbecue sauce as the first pieces sizzled on the grill.

"Ladies, ladies, let's pick up the pace, please!" Mr. Valentine said, clapping his hands for emphasis. "Our guests will be lining up soon."

At first, I thought he meant me and Virginia were moving too slow. Then I realized he was talking to Momma and her crew.

Good thing Mr. Valentine was a whirling dervish, constantly fiddling and fussing over his creations. He was too busy to notice the dirty look Momma gave him.

He may have been the caterer, but this was Momma's house, and she and the other women had been preparing things for the past day and a half. Nobody was going to tell her what to do or how to do it, not even a fancy chef from New Orleans.

"You're up, girls," Mr. Valentine said. "Bring me some crawfish. Quick, now."

Virginia and I grabbed a washtub and headed for the creek. We sprinted as fast as our bare feet would carry us across the rocky ground, the tub swinging between us.

We must have been a sight in our Sunday dresses and no shoes. Mrs. Valentine had tacked the hems six inches higher, so they wouldn't get wet.

We caught crawdads and tossed them in the tub as fast as we could. Thankfully, they were so thick in the holding pool that we could fish them out two and three at a time.

I stopped for a moment and marveled at how Virginia grabbed crawdads without hesitation. She obviously had lost her fear of them.

"What are you doing?" Virginia asked when she noticed me watching.

"I was just wondering how you got so good at this."

She smiled. "I had a good teacher."

It didn't take more than ten minutes to fill the tub and stagger back to the cooking station with the heavy load. We purged and rinsed the crawdads the way Mr. Valentine had shown us. Then we returned for a second batch to try to stay ahead of him.

When we got back, Mr. Valentine dumped the first tub of crawdads into the boiling water. "Voila!" he said with a flourish. "Three minutes and we'll be in business."

He let the crawdads boil a minute, then waved his arms to get Mrs. Prescott's attention. She was standing beside the table stacked high with dinner plates and silverware.

"Are you ready, Mr. Valentine?" she asked.

"I am, indeed."

Mrs. Prescott hooked two fingers in her mouth and let out a loud, piercing whistle. Everybody stopped what they were doing and turned to look.

"Supper's ready!" Mrs. Prescott hollered. "Come and get it!"

Folks got up and surged toward Mr. Valentine's cooking station. He was soon scooping crawdads onto the serving platters as fast as he could go.

He leaned toward us as he worked. "More crawfish, please, and keep them coming."

Virginia and I were off to the creek and back again and again. With each load, Virginia jotted down an estimate of how many crawdads were in the tub, so Mr. Valentine would know how much to pay me.

We must have caught and purged and rinsed eight or nine tubs of crawdads before things slowed down enough to take a break. Virginia and I flipped over a couple of washtubs and sat down. It felt so good.

It was almost six o'clock. That was when the switch would be turned on to start electricity flowing into the valley.

Waiting for this day had been like waiting for Christmas. Only much harder. After all, Christmas came every December. Electricity came only once in a lifetime.

At five minutes to six, Daddy jumped into the back of his truck. It was time for the big speech. He had been practicing it for more than a week. I'd even heard him reciting it to the cows as he milked.

"Attention! Your attention, please!" Daddy shouted. He

waited for folks to quiet down, but they were too busy talking, and it was nearly impossible for anyone to hear him over the commotion.

Daddy scratched his head. He reached down and grabbed an empty gas can and a chunk of wood in the bed of his truck. He held up the can and struck it repeatedly with the wood.

Bang! Bang! Bang!

The sound reverberated in the air and sent the birds in the trees flying and squawking. Everything else got quiet.

"Hello, neighbors!" Daddy began. "Thank you for coming. My family and I welcome you to our farm. More importantly, your electric cooperative welcomes you on this very special day."

His words brought a polite round of applause.

Daddy put down the gas can and chunk of wood before continuing. "Most of us have called this valley home for a long time. The only life we've known is one without electricity. That ends today!"

The crowd let out a cheer. Many folks jumped to their feet, clapping.

Daddy turned toward the barn and outstretched his arm, gesturing to the enormous lightbulb hanging above the barn doors just for this occasion.

"In a few, short minutes," he said, "we will witness a momentous transformation …"

The crowd suddenly cheered louder than before, its roar drowning out Daddy in mid-sentence. He stopped, a puzzled look on his face. Everybody was on their feet now, cheering, hollering, and clapping wildly. The band joined in with a lively tune and some folks started to dance.

Daddy watched in awe a moment, then turned and looked behind him. Someone had flipped the switch early. The electric lightbulb was on—big and bright and beautiful.

Chapter 35

THE SECRET IS OUT

Folks seemed to lose interest in food after the electricity came on. I suppose they were too excited and too busy celebrating.

Can't say I blamed them. I was so thrilled that my insides bubbled like a shook-up bottle of soda pop. The feeling made me want to dance and shout like everyone else, but there was still work to do.

Late-comers continued to trickle past Mr. Valentine's cooking station for a while longer. Fortunately, the line dwindled and disappeared before the crawdads did. But it was close. The last tub had taken Virginia and me forever to fill because the holding pool was nearly empty.

"Let's call it a day," Mr. Valentine said, turning off the burners on his grills. He scooped out the final batch of crawdads and arranged them on the serving platters between the last of the barbecued chicken and beef.

Virginia and I cleaned up while Mr. Valentine packed away his equipment and supplies. The work went quickly, probably because the music and watching folks celebrate provided a pleasant distraction.

When we were finished, Mr. Valentine mopped his face with a hanky, then pulled out an envelope. "This is for you," he said, handing it to me.

The envelope was thick and heavy. My name was scribbled across the outside, and orange, spicy-smelling fingerprints dotted the envelope where Mr. Valentine had handled it.

"Go ahead. Open it," he said.

I tore off the end and looked inside. I'd never seen so much money in my life.

"Wow!" I exclaimed.

"Hope you don't mind. I had to use some paper money. I didn't have near enough coin."

"No. No, I don't mind." I wanted to say more—something to match the marvelous feeling warming my insides—but my thoughts were swirling so fast all I could think of to say was, "Thank you!"

"No need for thanks, Ruby. You earned it," he said. "Now, why don't you and Virginia get something to eat. You must be hungry."

Come to think of it, I was starving. And worn out. My arms were sore from pumping water, and my feet and legs ached from running back and forth across the rocky ground.

There was plenty of food left, though the desserts had been mostly picked over. I didn't mind. I was hungry enough to eat almost anything.

Virginia grabbed an empty plate. I grabbed two. It didn't take long to fill them to overflowing.

"Look over there," Virginia said. "It's Paul."

Him again? I looked up. Yup, there he was. Of course, why wouldn't he be here? His family belonged to the electric co-op.

Paul sat at a table with Marty. Evidently, they had finished their work assignments before we did. They looked half-asleep with exhaustion.

"Well?" Virginia said, nudging me.

"Well, what?"

"You want to go over and say hi?"

"Not really."

"Come on, Ruby."

"No way. I don't want to embarrass myself." I was self-conscious about wearing a too-short dress, not to mention Virginia and I smelled a little fishy from all the crawdads.

"You seem to forget: You kissed his hog, Ophelia."

"So?"

"So, you can't embarrass yourself much more than that," she said.

"Don't remind me."

A devious look flashed across Virginia's face. "Come on," she said, walking away.

Before I could object, she was weaving through the maze of people and tables toward Paul and Marty. There was nothing I could do but follow.

"Look what the cat dragged in," Marty said, giving me the stink eye.

"Very funny," I said.

Marty wiped a smear of sauce off his mouth with the back of his wrist. "Hi, Virginia. Have a seat." He patted the chair next to him.

"Don't mind if I do," I said, sitting in the chair just to spite him.

Virginia sat down beside Paul.

"Do you really have to sit there?" Marty asked, scowling at me. "You smell like fish."

"It's crawdad perfume," I said.

Paul pretended not to smile.

"Did you boys have a good day?" Virginia asked, changing the subject.

Marty looked up as if about to answer, but then seemed to change his mind. He grunted and went back to eating.

"It went fast," Paul said.

"Yes, it did, didn't it?"

I hated small talk. It was so pointless. Fortunately, I didn't have to sit and listen to much of it. I saw Daddy coming our way. I'd been expecting him. He was going to give Virginia and her daddy a ride back to Crossroads. While he was there, he would pick up my secret surprise at Mr. Abbott's store.

"Hey, here comes Daddy," I said.

Daddy smiled and waved to folks as he made his way toward us. He looked tired and frazzled.

"I'll be leaving in ten minutes," he told me and Virginia, barely slowing down. He kept right on walking.

"Okay, we'll be ready!" I shouted after him.

Virginia and I gobbled the rest of our food, then ran to the house to get our things. She grabbed her tote out of my bedroom, and I got my jar and added the money Mr. Valentine had paid me. I didn't have time to count it, but I knew there was more than enough money now.

Daddy was waiting for us at Marty and Paul's table. He was working on a plateful of chicken, crawdads, and Momma's fruit salad. I figured it was the first he'd had to eat since breakfast.

"Got everything?" Daddy asked Virginia, inhaling the last of his chicken.

"Yes, sir."

"Good," he said. He stood up and wiped his mouth and fingers. "Ruby, I should be back in twenty minutes. I'll meet you here. Sound like a plan?"

"Yes, Daddy." I handed him my money jar.

He gave me a wink.

Virginia smiled and hugged me. She knew the dual purpose of Daddy's trip to Crossroads. "Wish I could be here to see everyone's faces. You'll have to tell me all about it," she said. "See you later."

"Bye!" I chirped excitedly.

Daddy and Virginia weren't gone for more than five minutes when Ed came running up to the table where Marty, Paul, and I sat working on our second or third helpings. He was out of breath.

"You seen Daddy?" Ed asked.

"He went to Crossroads," I said. "Should be back in fifteen or twenty minutes."

"Can't be soon enough! The Harpers' truck won't start." Ed had a toolbox in each hand. "Don't know if Daddy can fix it or not, but he knows a lot more about engines than me, and Mr. Harper is madder than a wounded bear."

"I'll let Daddy know."

"Thanks, Ruby." Ed turned to Marty. "I need you to go get Daddy's creeper for me. You know, the thing with wheels for crawling under a truck."

"But ..."

"I don't want to hear it, Marty. Just do it—please. Meet me in the pasture. You shouldn't have any trouble finding me. Just listen for Mr. Harper's hollering."

Ed hustled off toward the pasture while Marty slow-walked to the shop. That left Paul and me alone at the table.

Talk about uncomfortable! The only good thing was we still had food on our plates, so we didn't feel any pressure to talk for the first few minutes. The awkwardness started once we finished eating. After that, it was pure agony.

Paul finally broke the ice. "I hear you found Crawdad Haven."

"Uh, yeah. I did." I was surprised Paul had heard about that.

"I thought maybe you could show me."

"Sure. I suppose."

"Swell."

"But only under one condition."

Paul gave me a sideways look. "What? I have to keep the location a secret?"

I shook my head.

"What then?"

"No more punching me in the shoulder."

Paul looked away, but I could tell he was embarrassed. "Oh, that. Sorry, I do that without thinking when I like someone."

I was glad Virginia wasn't around to hear him say that. I could hear her now: "I told you so."

"So, is it a deal?" I asked.

"Deal," he said, smiling. And then, believe it or not, he almost punched me in the shoulder again. Fortunately, he caught himself, unclenched his fist, then put his hand on my shoulder.

His touch was warm and gentle, and caught me by surprise. It sent a wonderful jolt through me like nothing else I'd ever felt before But it also made me jump.

Paul quickly pulled his hand away and slipped it into his pocket.

I wanted to apologize and explain why I jumped. Truth be told, I liked his touch and wanted to tell him so. But I didn't have the nerve to say it.

"I can show you Crawdad Haven now, if you like," I said, aware of the blood rushing to my cheeks.

His face lit up. "Lead the way!"

The tour of Crawdad Haven was a quick over and back. No more than fifteen minutes, tops. The huge congregation of crawdads was long gone, but at least I could point out the piles of carcasses where the critters had snacked on crawdads.

Paul and I got back to the table just as Daddy drove up. My heart soared. I was all smiles as I ran to the truck.

"Hey, Daddy!"

Daddy wore a frown as he got out of the truck. It was a look that sucked the excitement out of me.

"What's wrong?" I glanced in the back of the truck. "Where is it?"

"Honey …"

"Where's Momma's surprise?"

Daddy grabbed something from behind the seat. It was my money jar. Not a penny of it had been spent.

"I know how much you had your heart set on getting your Momma that washing machine, but somebody else bought it, honey." He handed me the money jar.

I blinked hard, trying to comprehend. This was not at all how it was supposed to happen. I looked at Daddy and then at the jar.

"A washing machine?" Marty yelped, shaking his head in disbelief. He and Paul must have followed me. "You saved all your money for that? That's your big secret? What a joke."

"Martin!" Daddy barked.

"I know, I know. Come on, Paul." As Marty walked away, I heard him say, "Don't that beat all? A stupid washing machine."

I didn't expect Marty to understand. After all, he didn't seem to notice or care about Momma's hands or anything else. None of the boys seemed to care.

But I did. Ever since I was little, I wanted to make her hands look new. No more itch or hurt or ugliness. That's all I wanted. And I know she wanted it, too. She just didn't like to complain.

Daddy gave me a pained smile. "I asked Mr. Abbott to order you another one. He said he has a line on a similar model, only newer. Should be here in a few weeks."

That sounded reasonable enough. But I wasn't exactly feeling reasonable at the moment. I was mad.

"Who bought it?" I growled. I don't know why I asked. What was I going to do? Knock on their door and tell them I wanted it back?

"Mr. Baxter."

Daddy's words knocked the air out of me. I couldn't believe my ears. "For real? Mary Belle's daddy?"

He nodded. "Bought it this morning."

It felt like I had been punched in the gut.

Mary Belle must have had something to do with it. I just knew she did. She probably told her daddy to buy the washing machine to spite me.

But how did she find out?

I didn't know whether to scream or cry, but I was to the point where one or the other—or both—was going to happen. I had to get away. Now! And I knew just the place to go.

Chapter 36

WRONG ALL ALONG

My favorite place in the whole world was the ledge. It was a chunk of rock that stuck out of the face of the ridge like a gigantic tongue. On a clear day, I could see all the way to the river and beyond.

Daddy called the ledge his little bird's perch. I didn't know what to think of the comparison. An eagle maybe, or an owl, but I didn't see myself as a *little* bird.

The ledge was a special place. It was the perfect destination when I had thinking to do or when my spirits soared or plunged. Like now, after hearing the disappointing news that Momma's washing machine was gone.

Part of the magic of the place was the effort to get there. It was at the top of a steep trail that switched back and forth up the ridge like a zigzag stitch. The hike allowed me to let off steam as I climbed.

That's not how it worked this time. When I got to the top, I was still seething with anger. I picked up a rock and heaved it with all my might. I listened as it pinged off the boulders and trees below. It felt good, so I threw another one, and then lots more. By the time the anger was gone, my arm felt like I had thrown half the mountain.

I realized things would be all right—eventually—just as Daddy had tried to tell me. I had earned and saved more than enough money to buy Momma any washing machine she wanted. I just had to wait a little longer, that's all.

I sat on a flat rock mindlessly picking pebbles out of the ground, watching the gathering at our farm below. The crowd had dwindled. Those who remained stood around in huddles, probably catching up on the latest gossip or waiting for permission to nab leftovers to take home.

As I watched, a person left the gathering and headed across the farmyard, getting farther and farther away from everybody else. It was someone in a dark blue dress, too far away to identify. She was a woman, not a girl, but it wasn't Momma. That much I could tell.

Whoever it was crossed the bridge and followed the dirt track that led to the upper pastures. When she turned off at the junction with the trail, I realized she was coming up here.

But why?

I squinted, trying to make out who it was. I dropped the pebble in my hand and stood up for a better view.

She disappeared into the stand of trees at the base of the cliff. But I knew the trees would soon give way to low-lying brush and rocks where it was too steep for trees to grow. Then I would be able to see who it was.

When the woman came into view again, my chin dropped. It wasn't a woman at all. It was Mary Belle.

Why was she coming up here? For that matter, why was she at the co-op picnic at all? She didn't live in the valley anymore. She already had electricity.

Perhaps she wanted to gloat about her daddy buying Momma's washing machine. Yes! That must be it. She was coming to taunt me.

Anger welled up inside of me again. My hands turned to fists. I felt like pounding her the way I'd seen her pound other kids. The thought of it suddenly made my anger turn to panic. I knew if anybody was going to get pounded, it would be me.

I felt a sudden urge to run. But where? I couldn't go up, and the only safe way down was the steep, narrow trail Mary Belle was on. And there was nowhere to hide.

Mary Belle would be here any minute.

"Think!" I told myself.

I looked for something—anything—to use to defend myself. I hoped it didn't come to that, but I wanted to be ready if it did. Unfortunately, the best I could do was a rock the size of a baseball. It wasn't much, but it was all I had.

Mary Belle knew I could throw hard. She might keep her distance if she saw the rock, and then maybe nobody would get pounded.

I paced back and forth on the ledge. Waiting. I would have gladly waited for hours if it meant Mary Belle wouldn't show up at all.

But that was not to be.

"Stop!" I screamed, holding out my hand like a policeman directing traffic.

Mary Belle froze.

"Don't come any closer," I ordered.

Now what?

There was an awkward moment when neither of us spoke. We just stared at each other, unsure what to do next.

I glanced over the edge of the cliff. It wasn't a sheer drop, but it was steep. Steep enough to hurt if you fell—or jumped while trying to get away.

Mary Belle took a step toward me.

"Stop, I said! That's far enough," I warned, brandishing the rock. My heart was pounding.

She stopped. "What's with the rock?"

"Never mind that. What do you want?"

"There's nothing to be afraid of."

"I'm not afraid."

Mary Belle smirked.

That made me mad. "Are you going to tell me what you want or not?"

"Just put the rock down, and we can talk."

I shook my head.

"Why not?"

"I don't trust you."

Her eyes went soft. "When have I ever hurt you, Ruby?" she asked, almost in a whisper.

She had me there. I couldn't think of a single instance. But I remembered plenty of times when she had hurt others.

"Well, what about that boy you put in a headlock? His face turned purple, and I thought you were going to pop his head off."

Mary Belle straightened. "Oh, him." She grinned, remembering the incident.

"Yeah, him."

"Do you remember why I had him in a headlock?"

"Because he pushed me down and got my new dress muddy." As soon as I said it, I felt like a heel.

"That's right," said Mary Belle. "I was protecting you. My best friend. So, I ask again, why would I ever want to hurt you?"

I didn't have a good answer, so I answered her question with a question. "Then why are you here? You don't even like me anymore."

"That's not true."

"Then why are you always saying mean things and giving me dirty looks?"

Mary Belle grinned and shook her head.

"What's so funny?"

"I wasn't doing those things to you."

"Oh, no?"

"No. It was your friend."

"Virginia?"

"Yeah. Her."

It didn't make any sense.

"Why would you do that?" I asked, wondering how anyone could not like Virginia.

Mary Belle looked away, but not before I read the answer on her face. She was jealous. She didn't like that Virginia had taken her place as my best friend.

"I'm sorry," she said.

I shook my head. I was so confused. Before Mary Belle showed up, I thought I had it all figured out. Come to find out, I was wrong.

But that didn't change the fact her daddy bought Momma's washing machine, and she probably had something to do with it.

"You still haven't told me why you're here."

"I just want to talk," she said in a mousy voice. "I knew you'd be mad about the washing machine."

"You're darn right I'm mad! How could you and your daddy do that?" My throat tightened, and the last few words cracked as they came out.

"That's what I wanted to tell you. I didn't have anything to do with buying it. Besides, how could I know?"

She had me there. I'd only told Virginia and Daddy my secret, and they would never tell. She must have overheard me talking to Virginia about it.

"I don't believe you," I said.

"It's true," Mary Belle urged. "Momma's old, gas-powered washer died in March. She tried to make do and started washing the laundry by hand. Her hands looked terrible after a while. They got red and rough and ugly. You know how I mean."

I nodded. It was the same reason I wanted to buy Momma a washing machine. The more Mary Belle talked, the worse I felt about the mean things I had thought or said about her.

"Momma didn't complain. It was daddy. He felt so bad for momma he bought the washing machine," Mary Belle said. "He didn't know you were going to buy it. Me neither. Honest. Not until I ran into Paul at the picnic and he told me you were upset about it."

What she told me was so different from what I had pieced together in my head.

"Is that for true?" I asked.

Mary Belle nodded and crossed her heart.

I dropped the rock.

"So, how'd you know I was here?" I asked.

"Paul told me you were upset and ran off. I knew where to find you."

"But why were you at the picnic? You're not a co-op member."

Mary Belle grinned. "I know. When I heard there was going to be a picnic, I asked Wilbur Hanks if I could come along as his guest."

"And he said yes?"

"Uh-huh. I think he's sweet on me," she said, tossing her hair.

"Or maybe he was afraid he'd get pounded if he said no."

She giggled. "Maybe."

We both laughed.

"We had some good times, didn't we?" I asked.

"Sure did."

"Thanks, Mary Belle."

"For what?"

"For putting that boy in a headlock and standing up for me all those other times."

"You're welcome," Mary Belle said, blushing. "So, you're not mad?"

"No. Not anymore."

"Maybe we can be friends again?"

"Yeah, sure. Maybe."

She perked up. "How about now?"

I frowned. "Don't push it, Mary Belle." Almost immediately, I realized the words had come out wrong. "I mean, it's probably too soon, you know. For one thing, you have to get over not liking Virginia."

At first, Mary Belle didn't respond. Then, she smiled and said, "I suppose you're right."

"Maybe then we can be friends. Okay?"

She nodded.

There wasn't much else to say.

"Well, guess I better be going," Mary Belle said, waving. "Bye, Ruby. See you later."

"Later, Mary Belle."

By then, the sun was starting to set, but I was in no hurry to go home. A full moon would be rising soon. There'd be plenty of light to find my way down the trail.

I sat and pondered everything that had happened today. There was so much to think about.

It was dark before I knew it. Stars shone like glitter in the sky. Below me, the band had stopped playing, and more and more cars were leaving the picnic. They looked like beetles with headlights as they scurried across our farmyard, then turned onto the valley road, heading off in one direction or the other.

The moon was soon peeking over the ridge, signaling it was time to head home. Momma and Daddy would be wondering where I was. But then again, they probably already knew.

When I stood up to leave, I couldn't believe the scene spread out below me. It took my breath away. The star-filled sky appeared to be reflected in the valley below. But the bright points of light on the dark landscape weren't stars. They were lights at valley farms. Electric lights. More and brighter lights than any I'd ever seen there before.

It was a marvelous sight, reminding me of what today's celebration was all about. It was the first day of electricity in my life—and in the lives of everyone in the valley.

Chapter 37

WHAT NOW?

The front porch of Mr. Abbott's store was the perfect place to spend a hot afternoon. It faced east, and the chairs sat in full shade at that time of day. There was always a breeze, too, compliments of either Mother Nature or passing automobiles.

Usually, Henry would be there, but he was away on a salmon fishing trip up north. It was just Virginia and me today.

I was wearing my brand-new yellow dress with tiny white flowers. I'd bought it with money left over after paying for Momma's washing machine.

Truth be told, cotton dresses were cooler than overalls. Maybe that's why Virginia liked to wear them. Beats me why she was wearing overall shorts today. She had them rolled up just the way I wore them.

Our feet were propped up on a chair, with nowhere in particular to go. It was enough just to hang out together, drinking sodas and watching dust devils spin in and out of existence along the sides of the highway.

We were working on our second round of cherry colas—my treat. The empties stood beside my money jar. It was empty now, except for its bottom full of ten-for-a-nickel candy.

"Thanks again for the candy and colas," Virginia said, taking a sip. "And for *Caddie Woodlawn*. I adore that book."

"It's the least I could do."

"For what?"

"For all the things you've done and bought for me while I was saving for Momma's washing machine. And for just being my friend."

"Ahhhh, isn't that sweet." Virginia put her arm around me. "You're the very best friend anyone could have, Ruby Mae Ryan."

I put my arm around her. "You, too, Virginia ... ah, ah ... You know what? I don't know your middle name."

How could that be? What kind of person doesn't know their best friend's middle name? I felt so bad.

"No. No, it's okay," Virginia said. "I don't tell people my middle name. I hate it."

"Really? What is it?"

Virginia sat with her mouth drawn tight. "I'd rather not say."

"Come on. How bad could it be?"

"Promise not to tell anyone?"

"I promise."

"Prudence. My middle name is Prudence." Virginia wrinkled her nose after she said it.

Thank goodness I kept from laughing. "That's not so bad," I fibbed.

Virginia folded her arms. "Who names their child Prudence?"

"Could be worse. That could be your first name."

We both laughed.

A passing delivery truck sped by. The gust of wind in its wake blew Virginia's hair across her face. She combed it back into place with her fingers.

"Has your mother's washing machine been delivered?"

"Not yet. Daddy says it should be next week."

Virginia took another sip. "I'll bet she's excited."

"You can say that again, and not just about the washing machine. Momma started a wish list of electric appliances she wants to buy someday."

"Like what?"

"You know—refrigerator, iron, sewing machine, mixer. Daddy added a couple of things, too. The list is getting long."

"Oh, she'll love those things."

Virginia should know. Her momma already had all those appliances—and more.

Virginia nudged me with her shoulder. "Have you seen Paul lately?"

"Are you going to start that again?"

"Just curious."

"No, I haven't seen him. Why do you ask?"

"I heard you walked down to the creek with him—alone."

I squirmed. "Where'd you hear that?"

"A little bird told me."

"Well, did your little bird tell you there was nothing to it? Paul asked about Crawdad Haven, so I took him to see it."

"Uh-huh." Virginia smirked. "I told you he was sweet on you."

I was ready to change the subject.

"Did I mention I've decided to cut back on my jobs?"

"No, you didn't."

"Yeah, they take up too much time," I explained. "I'm twelve years old, after all. I need to goof off a little while I still can."

"Does that mean you'll quit washing Friday-night pots and pans for father?"

"Nah."

"How about ice runs with Mr. Abbott?"

"Probably, since there are only two weeks until school starts anyway. And who knows about next summer."

"How about crawdad catching?" Virginia asked.

"Are you kidding? How could I give that up? I'm the one and only Crawdad Champ, aren't I?"

Virginia giggled. "So, what are you going to save your money for now?"

I'd been thinking about that a lot.

"A car," I said.

"You're kidding."

I shook my head. "Nope. I want a big, fancy one. With pretty red paint and lots of chrome." I couldn't help but wonder how many crawdads that would cost.

"It's going to take a while to save that much money. Years," Virginia estimated. "Aren't there other things you want? Less-expensive ones, where you don't have to wait so long to get them?"

"Like what?"

"A bicycle, for one."

I used to dream of getting a brand-new bicycle, one of my very own. But that was before I knew what I really wanted.

"Nah."

"Why not? You can buy one just like mine. Even better. The new model has the headlight built right into the front fender."

"That sounds swell, but I've made up my mind."

Virginia wrinkled her nose.

"What?" It was more of a statement than a question. "If I buy a bicycle, I might be tempted to buy other things, too. At that rate, I might never save enough for my red car."

Virginia started to chuckle.

"What?"

She broke out laughing, slowly shaking her head.

"Are you going to tell me what's so funny?"

"What can I say, Ruby? You're one of a kind."

I smiled. "I wouldn't have it any other way."

Chapter 38

ONE MORE SURPRISE

Momma's washing machine arrived a month after the co-op picnic. The delay allowed Daddy to wire an electric outlet for the washer. He also hooked up an electric water pump and ran pipes to the back porch, so Momma could fill the washer's tub right from the faucet. No more pumping water by hand and hauling it to fill washtubs.

Mr. Abbott made the delivery when Momma and I were in Portland visiting Patsy. Boy, were we surprised when we got home!

The washer wasn't what you would call pretty. It looked like a headless, short-bodied hog. It was the size of a squatty rain barrel, and there were four white legs and black casters for feet. A cord curled out the side like a tail.

I about died with pleasure when I saw it, though. Momma did too. We didn't even bother to change out of our Sunday clothes to give it a test run.

Momma filled it with water from the new faucet while I ran and collected all the dirty towels in the house.

"Stand back," Momma said as she prepared to turn on the machine.

"Ready," I said.

The washing machine surged to life. We watched in awe as it vibrated and rocked gently in place, the towels and water churning inside.

Momma smiled and put her arm around me. "Thank you, honey," she said, pulling me close.

"You're welcome, Momma. No more ugly hands."

She looked at her hands, front and back. They were red, rough, and chapped, as always.

"They are ugly, aren't they," she said.

"Not for long."

"Why's that?"

"I'm going to make you some more hand cream," I joked, grabbing one of her hands and rubbing it between mine.

Momma let out a laugh. She nudged me and pulled her hand away. "Not if it smells like the last batch."

We both laughed.

"Momma."

"Yes, honey."

"I've got one more surprise."

Momma gave me a puzzled look. "What have you got up your sleeve, young lady?"

"You'll see."

"Wait a minute, now. I don't need another thing," she said, her voice cracking. "You've already given me the most wonderful gift I could imagine."

"You deserve it, Momma."

She gave me a hug.

"Stay right here," I said. "I'll be right back."

I turned and ran up to my room. On the way back down, I wiped my eyes before Momma could see them.

"Here," I said, handing her a package wrapped in a piece of newspaper. One of my hair ribbons was tied around the top.

A swirl of emotions showed on Momma's face as she studied the crudely wrapped package. "Whatever could it be?" she asked, holding the gift up to the porch window as if the sun would help her see what was wrapped inside.

"Open it."

Momma slipped off the ribbon and carefully unwrapped the package as if it were adorned in pretty paper worth keeping. I could see the anticipation on her face. When she pulled the final layer of paper away and saw what was inside, the anticipation turned to wet, shimmering eyes.

"Look at that," she gasped, holding it up to the light.

It was Momma's crystal vase.

Sort of.

"Don't laugh, Momma."

Momma shook her head. Her hand went to her throat. I could tell she wanted to say something but couldn't.

"I saved all the pieces—at least the ones I could find—and glued them back together. I know it isn't anywhere close to good as new, but at least it's not in pieces at the bottom of the outhouse pit."

In some places, you couldn't tell the vase had been glued back together. But in most places, you could.

The glued edges shone like razor cuts in the crystal. Tiny chips were missing here and there, too, but the way I figured it, the imperfections didn't matter. The vase would look as beautiful as ever sitting on its lofty perch above the kitchen window again.

"It's beautiful," she croaked.

I don't think Momma ever hugged me so hard or so long as she did then. I could feel her heart pounding and her body trembling, and I knew she was crying.

I wondered if she knew I was, too.

Afterword

A FEW MORE THINGS

When telling a story such as *Wish Upon a Crawdad*, there is rarely enough space to include every interesting fact or tidbit. Here are three topics with just such information not found in the story that you might enjoy before closing this book.

Underwater Gladiators

Crawdad, crawfish, crayfish, mudbug—whatever you call them, they are fascinating creatures. With their armored bodies and formidable pincers, they are the freshwater equivalent of gladiators.

Did you know crawdads are found all around the world? They come in many sizes and colors, including pink and blue.

But these common crustaceans have even more unusual traits. For example, most people don't know crawdads swim backward or that they can drown if there isn't enough oxygen in the water.

Which brings us to Crawdad Haven. Do crawdads really gather in large groups, as portrayed in *Wish Upon a Crawdad*?

The answer is yes; they do on rare occasions. Usually, it is because water and oxygen levels are extremely low. Crawdads can get bunched up by seeking out dwindling water and oxygen supplies. They may even leave the water to "breathe" air with their gills to get the oxygen they need.

The author had his own Crawdad Haven experience when he was Ruby's age. He and his brothers were exploring one hot, mid-August afternoon. The creek behind their house was low and still. When the boys came to a section in the shade of alder and fir trees, they discovered more crawdads than they had ever seen before—hundreds of them—covering the creek bottom and both banks. The boys couldn't believe their eyes. It was a sight they would never forget.

That discovery was the inspiration for Crawdad Haven and, ultimately, *Wish Upon a Crawdad*.

An Electrifying Idea

Have you ever wondered what life would be like without electricity? No doubt it would be more boring and a lot harder.

Without electricity, there would be no computers, smart-phones, game systems, or TVs. No electric lights, power tools, refrigerators, microwave ovens, or air conditioning. There'd be none of the millions of things powered by electricity that people take for granted every day.

Welcome to Ruby's world! She didn't have electricity for the first twelve years of her life. And she was not alone. When she was born in 1928, more than nine out of ten rural villages and farms in the United States didn't have electricity.

Meanwhile, most large towns and cities had enjoyed the benefits and conveniences of electricity for decades. That's because it was less challenging, cheaper, and more profitable for big, investor-owned electric companies to build and operate power systems where large numbers of people lived close together.

It was a different story in rural areas, where there were fewer homes and farms and greater distances between them. No surprise, it wasn't profitable to serve those areas, particularly while the country was in the grip of the Great Depression.

Fortunately, change was on the horizon.

In 1935, President Franklin Roosevelt created the Rural Electrification Administration by executive order. It was called the REA for short, and its mission was to bring electricity to rural America.

Congress passed the Rural Electrification Act the following year. The act made the REA permanent, and expanded its role to provide low-interest loans to build power lines and power plants throughout rural America.

Because existing power companies didn't share that vision, rural residents were determined to help themselves. Neighbors joined together to form their own small electric companies. They were called rural electric cooperatives.

Building power systems from the ground up wasn't easy. It took lots of money, hard work, and know-how. But rural Americans were not intimidated by the challenges.

They organized themselves, borrowed from the REA, paid membership dues to belong, and helped build power lines with their own hands. Many learned to wire their homes for electricity and helped their neighbors do the same.

By the time the country entered World War II in 1941, hundreds of newly formed electric cooperatives dotted the rural landscape.

Life would never be the same!

The arrival of electricity created an economic and cultural shift that was a boon for rural areas, as well as for the rest of the country. Thanks to electricity, co-op members could work night or day, produce more, and do it faster and more efficiently with electric tools and appliances.

After the war, many more electric co-ops were formed and existing co-ops grew. By the mid-1950s, the situation in rural America had changed completely. Most villages and farms finally had electricity.

Electric cooperatives are still going strong.

Today, there are 832 electric distribution co-ops in the United States. They serve approximately 42 million people in 48 states. Their mission remains the same as it was in the beginning: to provide safe, reliable, and affordable electricity to homes, farms, businesses, and schools where it once wasn't available—until electric co-ops came along.

Oregon's Hoover Connection

There is more truth than fiction in the chapter about President Herbert Hoover's visit to the fictional village of Crossroads, Oregon. He was no stranger to small towns or to Oregon.

Hoover had a tragic childhood. Born in West Branch, Iowa, in 1874, he lost both parents by the time he was ten years old.

After his mother died in 1884, he and his siblings were split up and placed with relatives. Eventually, Hoover was sent to Newberg, Oregon, to live with his uncle and aunt—Dr. Henry and Laura Minthorn—and their two daughters, Mary and Gertrude.

Interestingly, at the time *Wish Upon a Crawdad* takes place in 1940, Gertrude lived on the Oregon coast and very well could have been the cousin Hoover spoke of visiting in the story.

Hoover relished fine food, good company, and the great outdoors. He also was an avid sports fan. However, his favorite pastime was fishing. People who knew Hoover said he would rather fish than do almost anything else. He even wrote a book about the subject.

Hoover nurtured his lifelong love for fishing at hotspots throughout the country, including many in Oregon. He fished there as a boy, and returned to the state throughout his adult life to wet his fishing line in its waters.

Hoover enjoyed fishing the Klamath, Deschutes, and Rogue rivers. But his favorite river in Oregon was the McKenzie in the Willamette Valley. He had many fond memories of fishing its crystal-clear waters for trout, steelhead, and salmon.

Americans had a love-hate relationship with Hoover the president. Some blamed him for the country's economic woes. Others considered him a saint.

Hoover was president when the stock market crashed in 1929 and during the early years of the Great Depression that followed. As a result, his critics nicknamed ramshackle camps and shanty-towns Hoovervilles. Worn-out shoes with holes became Hoover slippers. Newspapers were called Hoover blankets because the poor used them in various ways to keep warm.

Supporters said Hoover was misunderstood and a victim of the times. They reminded critics that he was a steady, hard-working president who gave every penny of his presidential salary to charities or members of his staff.

They also pointed to Hoover's humanitarian work during and in the aftermath of World War I, when he led the crusade to feed millions of starving people in Europe. He was involved in similar endeavors after World War II. Those efforts won the admiration and praise of people worldwide and earned Hoover the nickname The Great Humanitarian.

About the Author

Curtis W. Condon has caught his share of crawdads. As a boy growing up in rural Oregon, he loved to explore the surrounding woods and lash together rafts to float a nearby creek with his brothers. Bits of some of those adventures found their way into this story. *Wish Upon a Crawdad* is Curtis' first children's book. However, he has been a writer and editor most of his adult life, including more than twenty-seven years at a magazine for members of electric cooperatives in the West. Curtis continues to enjoy the outdoors. His favorite activities include camping, hiking, beekeeping, and orienteering. He lives in the Pacific Northwest with his family and granddogs.

Made in the USA
Las Vegas, NV
16 February 2023

67638157R00152